Merryshields

The Island In The Attic

Jen Jones

Also By

Chronicles of Merryshields Main Series
Merryshields: The Island In The Attic

Chronicles of Merryshields: Stories from the Journal
Willow & The Hot Chocolate
Jack & The Exploding Planet
Piper & The Secret Story
Kit & The Ice-Cream

Buy
here
or from any retailers!

Join the magic at

Chronicles of Merryshields Newsletter

www.merryshields.co.uk

For Imogen, Eve, Freya and Brodie
With all my love

Welcome To Merryshields

Willow

I knew that Merryshields was the most magical place in the world as soon as I walked through its big, carved wooden doors. It might be the way it looks - it's a higgledy-piggledy old mansion, with little towers and gargoyles and big bunches of purple flowers hanging all over the walls. Or it might be the way I can smell hot chocolate when there isn't any there. Or it might be the sparkling sound of the fountains or the way the rooms feel as though something exciting is just about to happen as soon as you cross the threshold. But mostly, it's the way that Merryshields *feels*. It feels like it knows we're there, and it's happy about it.

I'm Willow and I'm ten. I'm number three in age now that we all live together, which is way better than before. It used to be just me and my sister, Piper, which made me the youngest all the time. Now we live here, with Jack and Kit, our cousins, so Kit's the youngest of us all, but he doesn't mind. Piper's the eldest - she's twelve - then Jack, who's eleven, then me and then Kit, who's eight. Our mum and Aunt Seren (Jack and Kit's mum) are sisters. We all moved in to Merryshields because our parents were planning to renovate it and start a hotel business, but *then* there was a global pandemic and we all got locked down (which means nobody's allowed to go anywhere or do anything). Uncle Peter lost his job because of lockdown, and now the Olds (that's what we call our grown-ups) are super-stressed and the four of us are staying out of the way. Piper says they're tearing their hair out, but I've seen no evidence of this.

Kit and I are currently playing noughts and crosses on the back of an old postcard we found. (I'm letting him win.) On the front of the postcard is a picture of a desert island, with a long, white sandy beach and some palm trees, and swirly white writing which says, '*Wish We Were There*,' which I think is the opposite of what it ought to say. While we play, Piper and Jack argue. They've been arguing for at *least* half an hour, but you should know straight away that it's not unusual for them. Jack's been winding Piper up, which he does for fun whenever he's bored. It started when he said she should go and find us lunch, but now it's become a fight about women's rights. Piper's tugging on her plaits - that's how you can tell she's really frustrated. Anyway, Kit and I have been laughing at them both for the last five minutes and they haven't even noticed!

We've been told that we're allowed to explore the whole house, which will take ages because it is MASSIVE. I'm really excited about it. Uncle Pete says even he hasn't explored properly yet. Aunt Seren said something about homeschooling because all the schools are closed and we are supposed to be doing our classes online. But we're quite relaxed about this because:

A) they haven't even got phone lines here at Merryshields yet, which mum says we need first before we can get Wi-Fi, and

B) most of our belongings are still missing, including all our devices, so we haven't actually got anything to do online learning on.

But just in case, as a back-up plan against doing any kind of school work, the four of us decided to start talking very loudly as soon as any of the adults mention it. And, if we're staying out of their way all the time, hopefully it'll never come up!

Piper and Jack are still arguing but it's getting boring now, so I stop listening.

"Willow, do you think we'll be able to explore every room in the house before we have to go back to school?" Kit asks me.

I pause. *I expect so, because this lockdown might actually go on forever*, I think. But out loud I say, "I expect so. It took Uncle Peter ages to just explore one bit of the house, so hopefully we won't go back to school before we're done."

"Some of the rooms are empty." Kit sounds disappointed about this.

"But loads of them aren't!" I say. "And it's an enormous house. It's got, like, three hundred rooms?"

Kit's eyes go really huge and round when he's surprised about something. They're doing it right now.

"Three hundred?!"

"That's what Dad said."

Actually, I overheard our dad asking why Mum and Aunt Seren thought they could manage this 'three-hundred-roomed monster' before we all moved in, but I don't tell Kit this. He already asks too many questions about where our dad is. (Before you start wondering, too, he's a doctor and he's got to work in New York - at least, that's what Mum says. Me and Piper think there's more to it than that, but Piper says Mum obviously doesn't want to tell us and maybe we don't want to know anyway, so we haven't asked any more questions.)

"Where is Uncle Toby?"

My heart sinks, but I hitch a smile on my face. "Working." I quickly change the subject. "So, anyway, I reckon we should count the rooms too, while we're exploring. Then we'll know exactly how many there are."

Jack's ears have pricked up. I think he's finally bored of teasing Piper. She's standing at the window, huffing and muttering under her breath, so I just carry on talking so that things sound ordinary. That way, she'll calm down. (I hope.)

"What do you think, Jack?" I call across to him. "Count every room?"

"We should make a map!" he suggests. "A floorplan!"

"Shall I get my scrapbook?" Kit looks eagerly at his older brother. "It was in the car with me and I haven't started using it yet."

"Sure. Find some pencils as well if you can."

Jack grins at me. He likes getting Kit to go and get things. He says it's because it makes Kit feel included and useful, but I think it's because Jack's a bit lazy.

I'd better explain where we are. We are in a room that is now known as Headquarters. The Olds started off calling it the Playroom, but we pointed out that it doesn't have any toys in it. They all looked pretty guilty about that. When we moved here from our old houses, the stupid removal company crashed their lorry with all of our belongings into a river. It upsets us all to think about it, so Jack quickly suggested that we call this room Headquarters instead ("It can be our base of operations!"), and all three adults looked relieved.

Headquarters is one big rectangle with the door at one end and an enormous window with a glass door in it at the other. There's a huge fireplace which we are forbidden to use, though Jack reckons he's going to negotiate for us to at least be allowed to toast marshmallows. (He's pretty persuasive when he wants to be, so we're actually quite hopeful.) On either side of the fireplace there are loads of dusty shelves, right up to the ceiling, and there's a cupboard built into the wall opposite, with a small wooden box inside it that is disappointingly empty. In the middle of the room, there's an enormous wooden table that could fit ten of me down each side. Apart from that, the room is completely bare. It even *smells* empty. I would never have thought that was a thing, but there you go.

Out of the Headquarters window, you can see the tree-lined drive - it's so long you can't see the road at the end of it - and a huge grassy area spotted with oaks. Mum says it's parkland and there are loads of deer here. Kit says if it's a park, there ought to be swings, but I don't think she heard him. If you were standing outside and looking back at the house, you probably wouldn't be able to tell which window belonged to Headquarters at first, because there are *so many* windows. Merryshields Hall is so big that Kit thought it was a castle at first. The building is really grand and it was built years and years ago. There are loads of odd little stairs and corridors and courtyards and things.

"I think the house is happy that we've arrived," I say.

Piper scoffs. "I think that's stupid."

She's obviously still mad. She might not think houses can have feelings, but I think Merryshields is special.

Jack's tummy is rumbling loudly. We are miles away from the kitchen, so I expect that when Kit gets back from getting his scrapbook, Jack will suggest that his little brother goes to find something for us to eat, as Piper clearly isn't going to go. It's been a long time since breakfast. Our first morning here, Aunt Seren made us all waffles in her new waffle maker and we had bacon and eggs as well - but since then, it's just been cornflakes.

Every day, the adults barricade themselves in two rooms on the other side of the massive entrance hall, up a flight of stairs and through two grand doors where they can't hear us and we can't hear them. They're calling it the Office Wing, which makes it sound a lot smarter than it really is. When they do venture out to spend some time with us, Aunt Seren and Uncle Peter end up having lots of quiet worried conversations in corners, frowning as they look around the house, and Mum mostly just sits on different chairs, looking sad. She'll try to look normal when we talk to her, but even her happy face looks sad. It's freaking me and Piper out a bit, so instead of engaging Mum in conversation and having to look at her sad-happy face, we just yell from a distance how great everything is, then wave and scamper away.

Truthfully, apart from Mum being sad, everything *is* pretty great. I mean, Merryshields is amazing, and we don't have to go to school, and we can't do any schoolwork - so basically, we get to do what we like. I'm really looking forward to spending our days exploring and having adventures. I mean, we've got no stuff to play with and there's nothing else to do. I'm certain that something special is going to happen here. I can feel it!

A Disappearing Tray

Jack

We have been in this house for approximately 3.75 Earth Days - which is 90 hours, if you find that easier to understand. Of those 90 hours, I'd estimate that Piper has been mad at someone for approximately 55 of them (once you factor in time spent sleeping). Right now, she's mad at me for suggesting that she goes to find us some lunch. She's sitting down at the far end of the table and is *still* messing about with her plaits - a sure sign that she's losing her grip. I suspect she is hungry despite the huge amount of cornflakes she ate earlier, so I have dispatched the youngest member of the crew - my brother Kit - to the kitchen to enquire about sustenance. He complained that he had already gone on a mission to get his scrapbook, so I promised him the last of the blackjacks when we find them. Blackjacks are a kind of sticky, chewy liquorice-flavoured sweet, and they're our dad's favourites, so they're a precious commodity in our family. Kit's eyes light up.

"Are there any left?" he whispers.

I nod, putting my finger to my lips. I happen to know that there were two left in the packet, so we'll both get one, but we'll have to hide them from the girls. It is important that we keep our strength up.

While we await Kit's return, we are discussing my plans for the house map. I have already decided how we should do it, but it's important to make your crew feel valuable, so I am letting them think they have a say.

I tell them we should start with an outline of this room.

"We shouldn't worry about the scale of the room yet," I told them, "because we don't know how many rooms we're going to find altogether, or how big they'll be in comparison to this one. So we'll just start here."

Willow says, "That's a good idea."

Piper shrugs and says she supposes it would work.

I open Kit's scrapbook to the first page, and grab a pencil from the grubby pile Kit found in a pot just inside the Office Wing. Then I draw an outline of the room. It's easy because it's just a big rectangle. I mark the door to the hallway and the door through the window, even though we can't use it yet. (Dad says we're not allowed to try, but I saw him testing the handle quite hard so I'm putting a pin in that idea - in my mind it's like a little flag, waving to remind me to try the handle out myself, sometime.) Me and Dad are quite similar, apart from the obvious distinctions - he wears glasses and is taller than I am. We both love blackjacks and we both like to test things out to see if they work, especially if you're not really supposed to. For example, once we tested Mam's new food processor. There was a power cut (maybe because of us), and when we came back from fixing it in the garage, where Dad had been explaining how the trip switch worked, we found that our blueberry smoothie had turned the whole kitchen... well, blue. Another time, Dad decided we should see if there was a fireplace behind the sitting room wall in our old house, so we got a massive sledgehammer and took it in turns to knock away the plaster - until half the wall collapsed, nicking the edge of a water pipe and turning the carpet into a mess of plaster-dust-sludge.

We both stayed out of the way for a while after that one.

My point is, I don't think Dad would *really* mind if we tried to open the door in the Headquarters window. I mean, he's so distracted with losing his job that it was probably just one of those things parents say automatically. You know, like, 'don't pick your nose, your brains will fall out' or 'don't open the attic window, your brother will fall out.'

Kit comes back from the kitchen empty-handed. Apparently, he's nervous of the new cook.

"What new cook?" Piper says. "We don't have a new cook."

"Maybe the Olds have decided to employ a cook so they don't have to worry about feeding us all the time," says Willow.

"No way would they do that," Piper argues. "Especially not without telling us. Besides, there's a global pandemic, remember? We all have to stay away from everyone else and we can't go into other people's houses. And anyway, there isn't any spare money since Uncle Pete lost his job!"

(She does tend to go on a bit if you let her.)

Kit volunteers to go and ask one of the adults about it, and we let him, even though it is a *Dangerous Mission*. I'm not surprised when he comes running back into the room less than thirty seconds later, saying how every one of the Olds are shouting into different phones and have angry eyes, so he backed out of the room before they saw him. A commendable decision.

"It doesn't matter who's in the kitchen if they're willing to feed us," I say reasonably.

Piper snorts. "There's probably nobody even there."

"I'm not lying!" Kit kicks the table leg as he walks past it and flops back into his seat.

I'm surprised at this little fight. Piper usually takes Kit's side for everything, and Kit usually forgives Piper for everything in return. They're normally thick as thieves.

I diagnose imminent starvation.

Willow stands up and folds her arms across her chest. She stares meaningfully at her sister, lips pursed.

Eventually, Piper says, "If someone is in the kitchen, it's because the Olds have let them be there."

Kit smiles into his lap and accepts this as her apology for not believing him.

"Right," says Willow, marching towards the door. "If none of you are going to go down there..."

We all wait in silence. I, for one, am listening for screams.

Willow returns with a red face and slides a huge tray of food onto the table. "Mrs Boudry says to eat up!" she announces. "She's the new cook," she explains when she notices our quizzical expressions.

We all jump up and examine the goods. There is an enormous pie with a golden crust, a lot of cold boiled potatoes sprinkled with something green and a crispy, colourful salad. There's also a jug of water with clinking ice cubes and four cups, but only one knife and fork. I raise an eyebrow at Willow.

"I'm not going back down," she says before I can say anything.

Kit picks up a cold potato and takes a big bite out of it. It is the most outrageous thing I have ever seen him do! He's not a fussy eater for an eight year old, but for some reason potatoes (which are a major food group of deliciousness, if you ask me) are Kit's arch nemesis. He doesn't like cheesy mashed potatoes, buttery jacket potatoes, crispy roast potatoes - he's not even that keen on chips. But his least favourite of all the potatoes is a boiled potato, and his least least favourite is a cold one.

This confirms my earlier diagnosis. Only being truly ravenous would make Kit voluntarily eat a potato.

"I'll go," I volunteer. To everyone else, this makes me look selfless, but I have seen Kit's fingers and I don't fancy taking my chances with whatever is living under his nails. Also, I must admit I am curious about the cook.

But the kitchen is empty when I get there. It's a gigantic room. It's even got two doors, one from the inside and one that goes to the outside. The entire room is the size of our old kitchen and our living room *and* our garden, combined. It'd be perfect for setting up all the chemistry kits Auntie Percy got me for Christmas that Mam kept saying we didn't have space for (though I think she meant she didn't want me to make loads of mess). In this kitchen there's room to make *loads* of mess, but then I remember it doesn't matter anyway because the science kits went into the river with the rest of our stuff.

I get the cutlery really slowly and hover by the door for a while in case this Mrs Boudry comes back, but I'm too hungry to wait any longer. I want to tease Willow and ask her where she found all the food, but it is clear that there must be an actual cook in the house because:

1. Mam doesn't eat meat.

2. Auntie Percy doesn't cook.

3. Dad hasn't left the Office Wing in the three days since we arrived - and there's no way he'd leave an amazing ham pie untouched.

When I get back to Headquarters, I find Piper and Willow haven't waited for cutlery either. I sigh and start loading my plate.

"Maybe the Olds bought the food and left it in the fridge for us to find," Piper muses. "They've got a lot on their minds. Maybe they just forgot to tell us. That's more likely than them hiring a cook."

Kit scowls at her, but his mouth is full of tomato, so he can't get any words past his bulging cheeks.

"There's obviously someone cooking," I say, but privately I am thinking that now Kit has eaten *two* things that he never normally eats, so there is definitely something weird going on.

Kit looks happy with me for backing him up. He shuffles a little bit closer.

The pie is really mega-tasty, even better than the dry-freeze space pie Uncle Toby brought me from America last year. The pastry is flaky and there's loads of ham. Even the salad is nice. Piper informs me that the wilted green leaves on the potatoes are mint. I'm suspicious at first, but it's actually edible. The leaves are minty but not toothpaste-y. It takes me less than five minutes to finish my whole plate. Four minutes and forty seconds, at a guess.

After lunch, we pile everything neatly onto the tray. Then we move to the other end of the table, near the window, and open the scrapbook to the page I started drawing on.

"The plan of the *whole* of Merryshields won't fit on one page, Jack," Piper informs me.

I inform her in return that I already know this.

"Perhaps we can put different rooms on different pages," Willow interrupts. She is the opposite of Piper because Piper likes to argue and Willow always wants everyone to be friends. "We can get loads of rooms done in one book."

"Um, guys," Kit says, pointing down the table. "The tray's gone."

There's a silence. He is right.

Piper stands up and starts walking around the room as though she is looking for it.

"There's no point looking for it," I tell her. "It's obviously gone."

"We'd have heard it if it had fallen onto the floor," Kit says.

"It was right in the middle of the table," Willow says. "It couldn't possibly have slipped off." She looks quite worried.

"Perhaps it was one of the Olds," I suggest. "Kit said they looked busy - maybe they came in here to get the tray, but were too busy to stop and talk."

Her eyes cheer up slightly, but she's still frowning.

"It's too weird," she says. "You know what they're like. At the very least, they would have asked if we'd washed our hands."

I frown. It *is* weird because I *do* know what they're like. If it was one of the Olds, they would definitely have said something to us. They are all obsessed with making sure we're alright. So there's no way they would have come into the room without asking. And I'm sure they also would have asked if we'd washed our hands before eating.

We all look at each other.

"It's a mystery," I say.

They all nod. It appears that, for once, we're all in agreement.

I smile. Solving mysteries is my favourite thing.

An Appearing Key

Piper

O bviously, the first thing to say is that this is going to be a very long summer, and we've only just had Easter. Not only is school going to be closed for *weeks*, we're going to have to spend our *entire* summer holidays here as well. No staying with Grandpa in Devon, no going to visit Granny in Scotland, and definitely no holiday abroad. (Mum said that wouldn't have happened this year anyway, even without the pandemic, because of Merryshields.) Dad will probably stay in New York... which is better than being locked down with him and Mum arguing all the time, but still. It's just me, Mum, and Willow, for now. And Aunt Seren and Uncle Peter, and the boys too, of course. But that's it. The only people we're going to see for months and months. No friends, no other relations...

To be honest, my cousins are alright company. Jack can be annoying but Kit is cute, even though I wish I could get to the bottom of this business with the new cook. I'm convinced our parents would have told us if they'd employed someone. Surely they can't have done, though, because all they've done since we got here is talk about how they're strapped for cash and the house is going to eat up all their money. No, the more I think about it, the more it doesn't make sense that they'd start splashing out on staff when we've never so much as had a cleaner before.

Mind you, before Merryshields, we all had ordinary small houses.

Someone clearly made that pie we had for lunch - or bought it, more likely - so I'm humouring Kit for now by going along with his imaginary Mrs Boudry. (Or should I say, *Willow's* Mrs Boudry - she's the one who named her, after all.) However, I'm sure that it was one of the adults who came in to collect the tray. After all, despite what the others think, apart from constantly telling us to wash our hands, they don't want to talk to us at all at the moment. They're always scuttling off to different rooms and they always stop talking when we come close. So it wouldn't surprise me if they just snuck in and snuck out again.

The only thing that's nagging at me is that I didn't *hear* them sneak in. The corridor outside this room is *really* creaky, and at either end of the corridor, there's a squeaky door. There's no other way to get here from the Office Wing, which is on the other side of the house. It's just not possible that I wouldn't have heard them coming.

So, it's what happens next that's really weird.

We decide to go with Jack's suggestion and start the map of the house by exploring the rooms directly around Headquarters, working outwards from there. As a plan, it makes perfect sense, although I don't want to inflate his already massive head by saying so. We begin with the room next door.

It is exactly the same shape as our Headquarters, which isn't the most exciting way to start mapping the house. The only thing that's different (apart from it having no furniture) is the fact that the door in the window actually opens to the outside. It took us about half a minute to establish this, plus maybe two minutes of trying to persuade Kit that we weren't going to explore the garden straight away.

All in all, we were in this room for about two-and-a-half minutes, max. I am ninety-nine percent sure that nobody went into Headquarters while we were out of it because I didn't hear anyone come down the creaky corridor or through the squeaky door.

But when we get back in there, there's something on the table that wasn't there before.

"What's that?" I ask. "Did one of you leave that there?"

Willow rushes straight over and picks it up.

"It's a key!" she says wonderingly, holding it up to the light.

I move closer, curious. It's small and golden, about the size of a front door key, but elaborately carved with tiny fish.

"What's that attached to it?" I ask.

It is a scrap of yellowish paper, with unfamiliar handwriting on. A faintly musty smell fills my nose as Willow twists it around to read:

Where is the lock that fits this key?

She looks up at me. "It's not Mum's writing," she says. "And I'm sure it's not Aunt Seren's or Uncle Peter's either. What do you think, Kit?" She holds it out for him to look at. "Do you recognise that writing?"

Kit shakes his head. "I don't think so. It's too swirly."

It is. It loops and curls as though it was written two hundred years ago, with a feather quill. We stare at it for a second until a loud banging at the window makes us jump out of our skins.

"Jack!" I snap. Of course it's Jack, bouncing around like an idiot. He must have gone back through the window in the room next door without any of us noticing. I shout through the window at him. "The door's locked. You'll have to go round."

He bursts in a minute later, laughing like a lunatic. "You should've seen your faces," he chuckles, clutching his sides.

"Shut up a minute and look," Willow says. She holds the key out for him to see. "This was on the table when we came in. Did you see anyone going along the corridor?"

"Nobody could have come along that corridor without us hearing them." He stops laughing and takes the key from her with interest. "Where did this come from?"

"That's exactly the point," I tell him. "We don't know."

Kit sidles close to me and I put my hand on his shoulder. "It won't be anything scary," I say to him, hoping I sound reassuring. "I expect it's just one of the parents, sneaking around."

Jack and Willow both shake their heads. Willow has a little frown between her eyebrows. She always gets that when she's worried. "Jack's right," she says. "They can't have done. Not without us hearing."

I open my mouth to reply but then notice something, in the scrapbook that's still lying open on the table, where Jack left it.

"Look," I say, and my skin goes cold. I don't want to scare Kit any further, but I have to show them. "Look, on the scrapbook... what *is* that?"

They turn around and Willow gasps. "A map!" she breathes. "It's..."

"It's drawn itself!" Jack says, going to the table and putting his hand tentatively onto the page, as though it might be hot. He's right; the paper is covered in thin, spidery ink, in a kind of dark-brown colour that makes it look like it was drawn a long time ago. Some of it is recognisable, like the tiny picture of the grand front entrance steps, but some of it doesn't look like it belongs to the house at all.

"But... but that wasn't there a moment ago? Was it? Did you see it when you picked up the key?" Willow's frown line is even deeper now.

I shake my head. "No, I'm sure it wasn't - I'd have noticed." I lean closer.

"Is that what Merryshields looks like?" Kit asks, standing close to me.

"It's... well, it's..." I begin, struggling to explain. "No, I don't think so," I say at last. "Because look - this is the bit that Jack drew earlier, that we labelled 'Headquarters,' see? But there's another door appeared, there, that isn't really here."

We all look at the blank wall where there definitely isn't a door, and then back to the map, where a door is clearly shown.

"And there," Willow says, pointing. "There's nothing joining up the Family Wing with the rest of the house, and the kitchen - that's *obviously* a kitchen, because of the table and chairs, but it's not the same as ours..."

"But there's someone in there," I say. "Look-"

"It's Mrs Boudry," Kit says. He is looking at the tiny figure standing beside the table on the map. "That's what she looks like."

I want to say that he can't possibly tell that, because it's just a teeny drawing, and besides, Mrs Boudry isn't actually real. But I don't know how to respond to this Mrs Boudry business, and Kit is looking pale, so I put my hand on his shoulder.

"There's a little dog, look," I tell him. "Right where you wrote that you want a dog!"

"And a palm tree!" Willow laughs, tracing the bending trunk up the side of the page. "Maybe there's one of those tropical gardens here somewhere!"

"It's way too cold for that," Jack notifies her. "It's an unusually warm summer now, but even so we're too far north for palm trees."

"Fine, then. What about *those* trees?" Willow asks, undaunted. She's pointing at a drawing of a little row of trees. "Are *those* okay here?"

Jack leans closer. "I think they're apple trees, so, probably," he concedes. I glance down at Kit. He has his finger on the little dog. I am just about to say something encouraging about the whole strange event, when Jack lets out a whoop of surprise that makes us all jump.

"LOOK!"

He stabs his finger against a bit of the map that I haven't looked at yet.

"What is that?" Willow asks.

"It's a box, I think," I say, squinting. "Or maybe..."

"It's *treasure*!" Jack yells, and Kit's eyes light up.

"It is!" he agrees, his eyes lighting up. "Look, Piper - that's a pile of gold coins coming out of a treasure chest, and that's a necklace or something..."

"Oh my goodness," Willow says, clapping her hand over her mouth and staring at me, her eyes wide. "Do you... do you think..."

"It doesn't mean there's treasure in Merryshields," I say firmly, not wanting everyone to get too excited and then disappointed. "I mean, someone would've found it by now."

"Would they, though?" Jack asks. "I mean, Dad says nobody's been here for years, and the estate agents told him they hadn't been able to survey the whole property. So there might be places that nobody's looked in for *decades*."

"I remember!" Willow says, removing her hand and flapping it excitedly. "I remember Uncle Peter saying that! And Aunt Seren said it was like the rooms kept moving around!"

I look back at the book. You certainly can't call it a map, since it doesn't seem to show a proper floorplan at all, but the more I look at it, the more it's obvious that it's definitely Merryshields, one way or another.

"The key must be connected to the treasure," Jack says, holding up the key again. "And this is a map. Well... it's *sort of* a map, anyway. We just need to find out who put the key there and ask them."

"But nobody had time to put it there and draw all of this," Willow says definitely, going back to the point. "There just wasn't enough time."

Kit looks from her to me. "Do you think Mrs Boudry is a ghost?" he whispers.

"No," I say firmly, at exactly the same time as Jack shouts, "Yes! That explains it!"

"I thought you didn't *believe* in ghosts," I say meaningfully. "I thought you said they're not scientific."

"Actually," he says loftily, "it was Auntie Percy - yes, your actual mam - who said that there probably is a scientific basis for ghosts. She said that scientists should keep an open mind about everything they don't understand, and I agree."

I widen my eyes at him, tilting my head towards Kit. Willow catches my eye.

"I think it's the house," she says. She clearly thinks this is a better suggestion than ghosts, but I can't see how thinking the house has produced its own crazy picture is much more comforting. "I think Merryshields wants us to explore, and it's showing us where to go."

"But it doesn't," Kit says, looking at the paper again. "It doesn't show us where to go at all. That picture of the treasure is just sitting there on its own. Next to a jaguar. It doesn't make any sense."

"Well, then," I say heartily, standing up straighter. "Maybe it's the house, or maybe it's just the Olds, trying to be exciting. But either way, it looks like it's just another mystery we've got to solve. Right, Kit?"

Kit looks to his brother for reassurance, and I glower at Jack over Kit's head. He looks slightly startled, but eventually catches on and grins one of his biggest grins.

"I love mysteries," he says, giving Kit a one-armed squeeze. "It's so exciting. I can't wait to see where this key leads."

Kit relaxes instantly, grinning back at his brother. I breathe a sigh of relief.

"Shall we go searching straight away?" he asks.

"I think we should make a plan," I say firmly.

Willow - the traitor - shakes her head. "Let's try the key in all the doors along this corridor, at least," she says. When I frown at her she loops her hair behind her ear and says earnestly, "Imagine if it is the Olds, and they've made a picnic, or got surprise ice cream or something? That's exactly where they'd leave it, isn't it? Somewhere nearby? And if it turns out not to be one of those doors, then we're no worse off."

I narrow my eyes at her, but she has judged it right - Kit jumps at the suggestion of ice cream, and the slightly creepy atmosphere in the room immediately dissolves.

"Alright," I say. "Let's go."

Silver

Kit

D rawing a map and writing the labels would be a lot better if I didn't have to help with the actual writing. Willow should do it because her writing is neat and tidy, but Piper says that my mam wants me to do handwriting practice if we're not doing school. And Jack says we have to make the Olds think we're being sensible. And Willow says she'll share her chocolate eclairs. So even though I hate handwriting, I'll do it. I'll get a pretty good sweet collection if I carry on.

I really want a dog.

Piper says that I'm not allowed one and Jack says even if I do, I shouldn't have written it on the map! But Willow winked at me, so she understands.

Anyway, I may as well tell you - I do want a dog. Mam and Dad said we might be able to get one when we moved, but then EVERYTHING HAPPENED and now we can't, which is really unfair. But nobody listens to me. I might as well talk to the walls.

Talking of walls, the walls down the corridor are a very boring colour. They're like green soup. I'm excited to try the key, but the first three doors are already open and those rooms are empty - and tiny. Jack says we'll still add them to the map, though. The next door is locked! But the key doesn't fit into the keyhole, even though we take it turns and all have try of turning it. The key doesn't open the next four doors either. Auntie Percy comes along the creaky floor in her flip-flops and asks if we're alright.

"Look, Mum!" Willow says. "Look at this amazing key we found!"

Auntie Percy doesn't know anything about the key.

"OOH HOW FUN!" she says, but I can tell she doesn't really mean it. She flip-flops upstairs again and we all look at each other.

"It's going to be hard to map the rooms we can't even get into," Willow says. She is looking at the door Auntie Percy just went through, so I know she is thinking about her mam and not about the map.

"I'm going to find a master key," Jack says. "That's a key that can open any door. It has a particular mechanism--"

Piper interrupts him by flapping her hand importantly. "I don't think there is one," she says.

Jack says there has to be, and Willow agrees.

"We can ask Mam and Dad when they get off the phone," I say quickly, before they start arguing. "Even though that might never happen," I add, very quietly.

"Good idea," Willow says. "Until then, I think we should just map the rooms we can get into."

So we put the key in the cupboard in Headquarters and start again.

This time, we go down the creaky corridor in the other direction. The first door opens straight away and then the strangest, most amazing thing ever in my life happens.

It makes me forget all about the key. It even makes me forget about Mrs Boudry. (Willow is the only one who believes me about her, by the way, which I think is so rude. Piper and Jack both think I'm making it up, and that Willow is just playing along to make me happy, but Willow said to me that she definitely saw her, and it <u>must</u> be the same person. She was the same shape as Miss Robbins at school, which is roundish all over, and she had a white apron with a big pocket. She smiled when she saw me, but she didn't say anything, and I wasn't expecting to see anyone, so I didn't say anything either.

I prefer to know ahead of time if unusual grown-ups are going to be in the house. Even an unusual house, like this.)

Anyway, the room we go into is DARK. The shutters are closed and we can barely see anything except the outlines of THINGS. It's sort of exciting and sort of scary, because I don't know what to expect. Willow tiptoes across to the window, arms outstretched to make sure she doesn't bump into anything, and opens the shutters so the light can come in. It's an old sort of study room, with two fuzzy green chairs and a spindly table with a book on it.

"This is creepy," Piper says, wrinkling her nose.

"This is *cool*," says Jack.

"WHY IS IT SO DUSTY?" I try not to touch anything. I'm pretty sure Jack told me once that dust is dead human skin cells and if the house has been empty for years, WHERE ARE THE DEAD HUMANS?

There's a big cabinet with glass doors, and Piper and Willow immediately start tweeting about some cute little ornaments inside it. Jack is walking slowly round the room with my scrap-book resting on his arm, drawing the outline onto a fresh page. He has what Dad calls his 'assessment' face - as though he is working out measurements in his mind as he looks at the walls and the window. As he walks past the desk, I notice something glinting in the sun, so go over to take a look. The piles of paper look boring, but on top of the desk is a little silver statue of a dog. It's smooth and cool and quite heavy, and when I put it next to my nose, the dog's eyes look right back into mine.

AND THEN, IT HAPPENS!!!!!

SERIOUSLY!!!

The little figure seems to dissolve into nothing, and I feel a cold nose against my leg. I jump about a *mile* into the air. Standing by my legs wagging its tail is the EXACT SAME DOG! It's sort of thin and bony, and silver in a furry way, and it has a long pointy nose that is looking at me RIGHT NOW! It's amazing. I'm calling it Silver. I think he's a boy.

There's only one problem.

"Hey! Look!" I shout. "It's a dog!"

The others barely even look up.

"It's really nice, Kit," Piper says.

"Maybe you could put it in your room?" suggests Willow, her eyes still on some old plate in the cabinet.

That's when I realise they think I'm talking about the little statue.

"No, *look*!" I say, pointing down at Silver. (I might have been a little bit DUH about it.)

"We get it. That dog thing on the desk is what your imaginary dog would look like," Jack says. He starts looking through the desk drawers. As though they would have anything more interesting than a DOG in!

So, that confirms it. NOBODY ELSE CAN SEE HIM.

It's a really annoying problem to have.

I sit on the floor and put my arms around Silver's neck. He's soft and wriggly and warm. He licks my cheek and it's actually wet!

"Hey guys," Jack says, completely ignoring the most magical thing in the world happening RIGHT IN FRONT OF HIM. "Do you reckon anyone's left important papers in here? Like lottery tickets or something?"

I can feel myself boiling on the inside like a volcano full of magma. Willow makes a funny face when she sees the wet patch on my cheek, but I don't know if it's actually because she can see that I'm about to explode lava all over the place. She's the most likely person to believe me, but I'm too cross to stay here any longer.

"Come on, boy," I say, and like THE BEST DOG EVER, Silver follows me with his long tail wagging, and we go back to Headquarters. I wonder if he's hungry. I'm going to go to the kitchen and see if there's anything I can feed him. I'm NOT taking him to mam and dad. They'll probably just take him away - if they can even see him.

Stupid Jack and my stupid cousins can stay in that room all night for all I care.

Silver Magic Spreading

Willow

P iper and Jack are having one of those hissing arguments out in the corridor. Piper is telling Jack to be nice to Kit and Jack is saying that his brother's taking it too far. Kit has dragged one of the massive beanbags from our sitting room upstairs into the corner of Headquarters and is slumped on it, ignoring us, his arm draped over something none of us can see. It's a bit awkward, really. We always play pretend games, but he doesn't usually carry on like this.

I go up to the Office Wing to see what Mum thinks of it, but when I get there, her voice filters through the door.

"Seren, did you speak to Glynis yesterday?"

I freeze. Glynis is our great auntie. She's about three hundred and smells of wee.

"No, but I spoke to the carer," I hear Aunt Seren reply.

"What did she say?" There's a pause and then Mum says, "Oh, don't make that face..."

"It's worse than we thought, Perce. She can't stay in the bungalow any longer. It's leaking, and--"

"Not as much as it's leaking here, Seren," Uncle Peter interrupts. "I found a damp patch on the wall yesterday the same size and shape as the Prime Minister!"

Mum laughs. Aunt Seren doesn't.

"Peter Fletcher, this is a ninety-two-year-old lady we're talking about." (Aunt Seren is usually quite relaxed about silly jokes, so I can tell she's stressed when she doesn't laugh and calls Uncle Peter by his whole name.) "She can't live there any more. It's ridiculous. And it's up to us to sort it out. She's family!"

"What about that old people's home up the road? Then you can pop in and see her whenever you like," Uncle Peter suggests.

"Peter, we can't put her into a care home, not the way things are," Mum sighs. "And besides, nobody's allowed to visit, are they? Everything is completely locked down." Mum's serious too now, which isn't a good sign.

"So what do you suggest? Moving her in here?"

My mouth drops open. He's obviously joking. They'd never let her live here.

"You're joking!" Thank goodness Aunt Seren says what I'm thinking. "She can't live here! It's cold, drafty, there's no central heating..."

"Just like her house, then?" Mum cuts in.

"Don't you start. We don't have any downstairs facilities, no accessible bathrooms... I don't fancy living with her, particularly, but the honest truth is that we simply *can't*, for her own sake."

There's a small silence. I'm just wondering whether I should come back later to talk to mum about Kit, when Aunt Seren starts speaking again.

"Have you spoken to Toby?"

Toby is my dad. My heart gives a funny little shiver.

Mum sighs. "No."

They're quiet again, and then Uncle Pete speaks in his too-jolly voice. He's been using it a lot recently. He hates seeing anyone upset when he can't make everything better.

"At least the kids are alright, though, eh? That's one thing we don't have to worry about."

"Yes, Perce," says Aunt Seren. "Keep that in mind. The children are fine."

Well, I obviously can't go in now, so I turn around and go back downstairs. I keep wanting to turn around and see if someone is watching me, which is stupid, I know, but my shoulders feel all funny. I shake it off.

Jack and Piper are in an empty room along the corridor, and Kit is still in Headquarters. I head back to the study and sit at the desk, which is really dusty smelling. There's a shiny patch of no dust where Kit took the dog statue from (I wonder where he put it) and a clock that says it's half-past six. It's actually almost right, although the minute hand isn't moving. It's a really pretty clock - I don't know how it works because it looks like it's too old for batteries, but I'm going to ask mum if I can have it in my room, since my clock went into the river and all. It's got tiny delicate legs and a smooth, shiny surface, and two little silver love birds sitting on a twig on the top.

They move.

The birds actually move! I'm watching, holding my breath, and one definitely lifts its beak as though it's smelling the air. The other one twitches its wing. I daren't breathe. The hairs have risen all along my arms.

"Kit!" I call out, as softly as I can. I don't want to scare them away.

He doesn't respond.

"Kit!" I try again.

There's a movement in the corridor and a funny, small, clattering sound. What if he misses it?

"KIT!" I finally shout.

I hear a shuffle and his footsteps as he pauses outside the door. He probably thinks Jack's in here. I keep my eyes fixed anxiously on the birds. They're not moving, but I think it's just because they've paused, not because they've frozen into statues again. The door creaks open.

"What?" Kit says.

I beckon at him wildly.

"Come here! Slowly!"

"No, thank you."

He sounds so sad that I have to turn around. His shoulders are slumped and he looks more miserable than I've ever seen him. Standing next to him, Kit's hand through his collar, is...

"I can see him! Kit, I can see Silver!" I can't believe it, but it's true. What is going on?!

"You're just saying that."

"No, I'm not! He's... he's got shiny black eyes and - oh, his claws! It was his claws clattering! And look - his tail's wagging! Just come here, will you? Something else in this room is alive too!"

A look of absolute joy flashes across Kit's face. He bends down and squeezes the dog, who licks his face affectionately, and then dashes across the room, skidding to a silent halt beside me. His eyes scan the desk.

"What is-? Wow!" His mouth forms a perfect 'O' of surprise.

We watch as the little birds stretch their wings and sidle along their twig. When one lets out a coo, I gasp, and they startle and flutter up into the air, then swoop across the room to land on the back of an armchair.

"This is amazing," I breathe. "Hey - Kit. Do you think he's the dog from the scrapbook map?"

Kit's eyebrows raise all the way up to his hair and he nods wildly, but before he can answer, Piper and Jack *finally* appear in the doorway. I can't believe they didn't come as soon as they heard me shouting for Kit - they're usually so nosy.

"What's amazing?" asks Piper, coming over to join us.

"The birds up there - they've moved - look!" I point over behind Jack, who's wandered into the middle of the room to survey us, hands on hips.

"Where?" he asks, craning his neck. Kit is giggling, waiting for them to realise.

"THERE! On the top of that cabinet!" I say.

"What, those two?"

"YES!" Kit and I shout at the same time.

"Aren't they just part of the decoration?" Piper frowns.

"NO!" we shout at the same time again. We look at each other and grin.

"I'm going closer," Jack says.

Piper leans over and whispers in my ear. "Are you just, you know, playing along to make Kit happy? 'Cos it's really not fair, if you are."

I look her straight in the eye, so she can tell I'm not lying. "No! I'm not, I'm really not, Pi! They were right here, look, on the empty twig! And look at Kit's dog! He's real too, can't you see?"

"None of us can see the stupid dog," she mutters.

"I can," I say.

Jack swears.

"JACK!" This time it's me and Piper who shout at the same time.

Kit laughs with glee. "Told you!"

Jack's grin is almost as big as Kit's and for a moment they look identical, even though Kit's hair is curly and sandy-coloured, and Jack's is straight and black.

Piper is shaking her head, but then she looks back up at the cabinet and claps her hand to her mouth. "Where did they go?"

Jack spots Silver and his eyes go really big. The next moment, he's on his knees, rubbing Silver's ears. The dog snuffles into Jack's hair, delighted at the fuss, his tail whipping back and forth against Kit's legs.

Piper suddenly freezes as she sees what Jack's doing.

"There's a dog," she says, stupidly.

"I TOLD you!" Kit cries. "This is Silver. He's a good boy, aren't you?"

Silver barks.

We jump, and then we all laugh and laugh - Kit out of relief, I think, that everybody now believes him, but the rest of us out of that odd kind of hysterical feeling when something happens that's so strange and peculiar that you have to shout or laugh or cry, just to use the energy up. When we finish, we collapse onto the floor and Jack points back at the cabinet again. The birds are perched on top of it, hunkering down into their silvery feathers.

"Right," says Piper, slightly breathlessly. "We need a meeting. Urgently."

"I wonder what else in this room is going to come to life," Jack wonders aloud.

"I bet there's something else off the map," Kit says.

We ignore Piper and eventually she stops wittering on about meetings and joins in looking at all the other things in the room, peering at the magical map to see if any of the other pictures match up with anything in the room. We stay there for an hour, until it gets too dark to see.

No matter how much we stare, nothing else moves so much as one dust mote on its own.

Things That Grow On Trees

Jack

We spend all the next morning in the study again, but nothing happens. Literally, not a tiny thing. Even the smell stays still. We're all hungry and bored and then Kit says he wants to take Silver out. I feel a bit bad about not believing him yesterday, about Silver. 'Specially since I thought I saw a flash of silver when he was in Headquarters. But it can't be helped. I'll just have to share my secret stash of refreshers later. He'll understand.

Last night, the Olds found us in the study and made us get washed and eat pizza. Somehow the cook subject didn't come up. None of the Olds could see Silver. Unsurprisingly. They did a lot of overenthusiastic, 'Oh what a lovely game! A dog! Ha ha, Kit, now you don't need us to get you one!' Silver doesn't seem bothered. He just sat next to Kit and ate his pizza crusts. They were pretty decent pizzas. Then they started talking about the old orchard that's on the west of the driveway. They said it was an orchard, anyway - you'd think it was just a massive overgrown jumble of trees and plants. So today, I say, "Shall we go and check out the orchard? I mean, there were trees on the map, so maybe it'll be interesting."

And everyone says, "Yes."

So we go outside.

We crunch down the driveway and run over the grass, Silver barking and Kit laughing as he chases him. Silver seems to know where he's going, which is odd, since twenty-four hours ago he was a statue. He leaps over a crumbling wall and we

climb after him, over the rubble. I feel like an explorer dis-
covering a new world.

The orchard stretches away further than I can see. The
trees shoot up like crabby, bent little space-gnomes, and the
grass is really long. There's lots of different sorts of grass I
haven't seen before - one blade that I touch is slightly furry.
Maybe it's space grass. (Dad would probably love to mow it
but - you guessed it - lawnmower's in the river.) It's April
and it's *really* warm. Brightly coloured flowers pop up all over
the place and bees buzz noisily. Silver's trying to catch a
butterfly. We wander amongst everything until we can hardly
see Merryshields at all. It's so quiet here. Like roads and cars
and rockets haven't been invented yet. There's just insects
zooming past my face. Some of them definitely look like aliens
- sort of like shiny greenish beetles with antennae. Birds are
everywhere. They make a lot of twittering noise. I bet it's easy
to build a nest here.

"Which one are you going to climb?" Kit asks. "I'm going to
climb this one."

I veer off to the right and choose a tree. The bark is all
grey and knobbly and it's warm under my hand. Smells like
sunshine and apples. I stand back to look at it for a moment,
pulling out my notebook from my pocket. Dad got us each a
notebook and pens from the nearest shop, which is like an
hour's drive away. I think he's feeling bad about the whole
all-our-stuff-in-the-river thing. He keeps pushing his glasses
up his nose, which is a sure sign he's bothered about something. I make a few sketches, considering the various angles of
the sturdiest parts of the trunk. If we get some supplies from
the house, I think we could build a pretty good treehouse.
It would take a few calculations regarding the strength of
different branches and their proximity to each other and the
ground, but it's certainly not impossible. I put the notebook
away and pull myself up into the tree, assessing as I go, but
what happens next drives all thoughts of treehouses straight
out of my mind.

"I wonder what kind of trees these are?" Willow asks, as Piper helps her up into the lower branches of a tree.

"Fruit," I grin.

"But *what* fruit?" I can almost hear Piper rolling her eyes at me. She's chosen a tree one across and two diagonally up from mine. It's very pleasing how the trees are laid out in a grid pattern, with only small saplings pushing up through the grass between them.

"Whatever fruit it is, there won't be any for ages," Willow says sadly.

We all climb as high as we can, entering into thick leafy obscurity before emerging into the blue skies above. I get to the top first and wait for everyone else to catch up.

Somehow, Kit's got Silver up next to him and all I can see is that goofy dog's face poking out from between the blossoms. I can hear the girls exclaiming in the leaves somewhere nearby and then Piper's head pops up into the sunshine and she's grinning so much she looks normal.

"What is it?" I ask.

"Jack, look at my tree!" she cries. "It's growing grapes!"

And I'm like, "So it's a grape tree?"

But then Willow's head pops out from a different tree and she's grinning all over her face too, and she says, "Mine's got plums! Look!"

I look at Kit. I can just about make out his face behind Silver's pointy nose. He shrugs. Not that I expect him to know why the girls are so excited, but you never know. He surprises me sometimes.

Piper stops looking normal and goes all grown up again. "Jack, you clearly don't understand. None of these trees should have any fruit on at all."

"Er, why?"

Willow is giggling. "Because plums don't ripen until nearly my birthday, and grapes don't even grow on trees like this! They grow on *vines*!"

I'm so surprised I nearly fall off my branch. "Do you think this is another *thing*?"

Kit's bouncing up and down so much that all the branches in his tree are shaking.

"Kit, stop it!" Piper calls. "You'll fall out!"

"Or Silver will," Willow says. Her head disappears again.

"My tree's growing fruit too!" Kit yells.

"What kind?" Piper asks. Her hair has got caught in the branches and one of her plaits is coming loose, and she has a greenish-brown smudge down one side of her face. It makes me smile as much as the fruit does. I start looking around my tree.

"I don't know." Kit sounds puzzled. "It's orange..."

"Oranges?" I ask.

"No, these are small... and sort of... soft. Velvety."

"Apricots!" yells Willow.

"Those things that Auntie Percy has?" He sounds doubtful. "Those are much squishier."

"No, those ones are dried," Willow's voice says. I can see her hair moving, it's a bit lighter than Kit's and I want to tell her it looks monster-ish because of the way the light is reflecting off the green leaves, but there are more important things to think of right now. Her head pops out again. "Throw me one," she says, and sticks out her hand.

Kit's got a surprisingly good throw, for someone who's three years younger than me. He chucks her the fruit so fast I can hardly see it move. Willow's pretty good at catching - better than Piper - but she nearly falls out of the tree and we all hold our breath while the branches wave wildly around. Eventually, we hear her voice again from somewhere in the depths.

"I'm ok." She sounds breathless. "It is an apricot!" She rustles her way up again and appears in a different gap, looking red, with a scratch down one cheek.

Piper is staring hard at all of our trees. "These trees all look the same!" she says. "They've got different fruit and they're different heights, but the leaves all look the same."

As she speaks, though, there's a sort of shiver across her tree, and all the leaves change.

"They're not the same now," Willow says, frowning. "Now they're massive. That's not right either."

The leaves droop.

"Don't worry," Piper says, patting a branch. "It doesn't matter if the leaves aren't right. We're still really happy about the fruit." The leaves perk up again. Piper smiles.

"There's still no fruit on mine, though," I say. I search all over my tree, but there are only curly yellow flowers on the ends of the branches. Kits starts feeding slivers of apricot to Silver, Willow says something indistinguishable with her mouth full, and Piper licks grape juice off her hands. They are obviously enjoying their trees more than I am.

"Hang on a minute..." I say.

"Wha'?" Willow swallows. "What have you got?"

I can't speak. I watch with amazement as fruit blooms at the end of the branch, looking more and more bizarre in our English spring sunshine. Then...

"BANANAS!" I shout. "My tree's the best. This is INCRED-IBLE!"

Pirate Spotting

Piper

*O*f course, Jack would go on about *his* tree being the most amazing because it has 'exotic' fruit growing on it, but luckily all his boasting doesn't detract from our enjoyment. It's like having a picnic up in the sky; bits of sun shining through the leaves and birds flittering between branches. We completely fill ourselves up on fruit. When we've each eaten lots from our own trees, we throw fruit to each other, so there is a rainbow of grapes, plums, apricots and bananas flying through the air. I only drop a couple of plums and one banana - though that's more than Kit drops, which is annoying. He doesn't drop *any*. It is honestly the most delicious fruit I have ever tasted. I've never thought of a tree having feelings before - that's a bit too weird - but I feel as though my tree is definitely happy to hear me whisper that its grapes are the best.

We all get really sticky and thirsty, and Jack is just trying to ask his tree for a glass of water (why he thinks that will work, I don't know) when I happen to look up at the house and tell the others to shut up and look, too.

From our nests we can see the front of Merryshields, with hundreds of windows shining in the sun. The entrance is big and grand, with double sets of steps curving up to the huge front doors. Everything to left of the front entrance is the West Wing, and that's the bit we haven't been to yet. The sticky-out bit on the other side is what we call the Family Wing – it's where we sleep and has all the family rooms in it. Merryshields is so gargantuan that I don't even know how far back it stretches, but somewhere there's a stable block. The

Olds are eventually going to convert the stables into holiday cottages, and we've been told to stay out of the way until the building work has finished. Apparently that's where all the money will be coming from, as soon as people are able to take holidays again - and as soon as the builders can start work, of course. I really want that to be soon because Mum said that Dad might stay in one of the cottages when he comes over, so we can see him really easily.

She *might* have just been saying that because of the whole probably-getting-divorced thing. I mean, Dad has mixed feelings about whether Merryshields can even earn income, from what I can tell, so I'm not sure he'd want to come here and prove her right.

Anyway, when I look up at the mansion, the sun is shining so brightly that I have to squint to see properly. It takes my eyes a few seconds to work out what they're seeing, and even then I don't believe it until I tell the others to look and hear their gasps.

In the very top window, at the corner of the house, are three bright red parrots, a big black flag flapping in the breeze, and an arm.

I swear my heart stops.

"It's a pirate flag!" Kit shouts excitedly.

"Don't be ridiculous," I say automatically, although that's exactly what I had thought at first.

Willow leans precariously back, one hand over her eyes. "What kind of flag is that?" she asks.

Jack, who had his back to the house, has to swivel around in his tree to see.

"Do you realise you've got a rip all down the back of your t-shirt?" I ask, rolling my eyes.

He peers up at the strange sighting for less than a second. "It's a black flag with writing on," he reports. "It says 'Help!' You can see when the wind blows it flat. Keep watching."

We do, and he's right. Annoyingly.

"We have to go up there!" Kit says. He's already scrambling down his tree. Silver is awkwardly trying to follow - goodness knows how he got up there in the first place. I look away, worried that they'll fall and hurt themselves.

"Hang on," I say, trying to turn myself around to get my feet in the right place. "We can't just go storming up there. Who knows who it is?"

"It's a pirate," comes Kit's disembodied voice from the tree. "*Obviously*."

"I mean, who it *really* is," I say, struggling out of a difficult gap. "It can't--"

"Don't say 'It can't be a real pirate'," Willow interrupts. "That's like saying 'it can't be real fruit', or, 'it can't be a real dog'." She is already on the ground - how has she managed that so quickly? - and is lifting Silver down to the grass. She makes a fuss of him and his tail wags so quickly it's a blur. "What I want to know is, how do we get up there? That house is like a maze."

"What I want to know is, how you got out of that tree so quickly," I mutter. My shirt has caught on a twig and I know if I jump it will tear, but I'm getting really hot and sweaty and irritated.

"What I want to know is, where's the nearest drink?" Jack says. He's on the ground, too, next to Kit's tree. "I'm about to collapse from thirst."

Kit clambers down next to his brother. "Ooh, I've got one! What I want to know is, does this now prove to you all that Mrs Boudry is real?"

We all look at each other.

"I already said she was real." Willow narrows her eyes. "I saw her too, remember?"

Silver trots over to Kit and nudges at his knee until Kit fondles his ears. "Oh yeah," says Kit. "I forgot. Anyway, I'm thirsty too. And hungry. For something that isn't fruit," he clarifies, before I open my mouth.

"Shall we go to the kitchen first?" I suggest, slowly. For some reason, the thought of finding out if Mrs Boudry is real seems more scary than finding the pirate.

"Good idea," Jack says promptly. So off we go.

It's absolutely *boiling* hot; if the adults see us they will definitely smother us in sun cream and make us wear hats. I wouldn't mind putting on a cap - Dad said he'd send us some from New York - but Mum likes us to wear huge floppy ones with big brims so that the backs of our necks don't burn. Because of this, we are careful to stay out of sight of the front door. The Olds are unlikely to be looking out of the windows, but we creep behind the soaring plane trees and hope that the shadows will hide us just in case. When we reach the gravel path, Jack, who is in front, holds out his arm and points silently ahead. We all peer round him to look.

"The kitchen is just beyond the family wing," he says quietly. "We'll be able to get to the outside door if we go round this way. Better than trying to go straight across the grass there to the front door. If any of them look out of the office window, they'll see us straight away."

Everyone makes a thinking face as they try to work out the inside of the house and imagine where it would fit from the outside.

"We need to finish that map," I puff, pulling at my sweaty collar. "And get out of the sun. I'm steaming."

"Jack's right," Willow says. Her forehead is all wrinkled and her eyes are closed; one of her hands is moving through the air in front of her. Her eyes snap open. "Yes, because if you go out of Headquarters, away from the main stairs but along the looooong passageway, the kitchen's through the creaky door and at the end of that little corridor. It's about five hundred paces." We stare at her. "What?"

Kit is the first to break the silence. "Five hundred?" he asks. "How do you know?"

"I counted them yesterday," she says, with a little grimace, "when I had to carry that tray all the way back to Headquarters."

"Right. Then let's see if we can get in that way," Jack says. "It means we can go in and out of the house without any of the Olds seeing us - we can add it to the map!"

"Better hope the door's unlocked," Willow says, crossing her fingers.

I glance up at the flag, still flying in the breeze, and nod. The arm and the parrots have both disappeared and I don't know if that makes me feel better or worse.

"Good idea," I say. "Let's go."

Mrs Boudry

Kit

We smell baking before we even get to the kitchen door, because the window is open. Luckily, the door is open too, so Willow's crossed fingers worked. I smell something oniony and something biscuity as well, and you'd think the two smells wouldn't go together but they do!

Piper goes first and stops so quickly that I walk into the back of her, and then Jack tells us to HURRY UP! because he thinks he's seen someone coming round the corner of the house. We all hurry in and I shout, "I *told* you!"

Mrs Boudry is standing *right there*. Her apron is blue this time and she's mixing something in a big bowl.

Willow waves. "Hi, Mrs Boudry!"

Mrs Boudry smiles and says, "Hello children!"

I can't believe she actually replies! At first, I think Piper is going to ask who she is, but she doesn't. She goes extra-polite, which makes me and Jack chuckle.

"Excuse me, Mrs Boudry, sorry to bother you but please may we get ourselves something to drink?"

Willow gives Piper a funny look - it is our kitchen, after all, and we only want water.

"Of course, my dear. Go and sit down and I'll bring you something over." We all sit at the table. Mrs Boudry adds, "I'll just pop to the pantry," and I am just about to ask what a pantry is when she WALKS RIGHT THROUGH THE WALL!!!!

We are all stunned into complete silence. We don't even move. We just stare at the spot where she vanished.

"Uh... You all saw that, right?" asks Jack.

Then she comes back with four glasses stacked on top of each other and a big glass bottle. THROUGH THE WALL AGAIN! She puts them on the table, one in front of each of us, and pours out the liquid.

It's fizzy, so I know I'm going to drink it, but the others just sit there with their mouths open. So I say very loudly, "The ham pie was delicious, Mrs Boudry, thank you very much!" so that they remember that they've already eaten her food and she probably isn't going to poison us.

She gives me a big smile and says, "You're very welcome, my young man." Then she looks at Silver. "I expect your dog could do with a bowl of food, too."

"Yes, he could, please," I reply, and she disappears back through the wall. Silver tries to follow but he bumps his nose.

As soon as she's gone, Piper hisses at me, "What are you doing?" She obviously doesn't understand.

"I am drinking fizzy lemonade and it is yummy, thanks for asking. I'll drink yours too if you don't want it?" I hold out my hand to take her glass but she doesn't move. I grin.

"I thought Silver might walk through the wall too, then," Jack mumbles.

"Don't be silly!" I'm a bit shocked that Jack would suggest something so unlikely. "He's a dog." *Anyone* can see that Silver is a proper dog and not a ghost, which is obviously what Mrs B is. And now that I'm here in the kitchen with everyone, that thought isn't half as scary as when I first thought it, in Headquarters.

Willow is looking very thoughtful, but at least she has started sipping her drink. "This is amazing lemonade," she says.

Piper opens her mouth to say something but Mrs Boudry comes back with a dog bowl full of meaty-smelling stuff for Silver. She even tells him to SIT before she puts it down, and he does! So now I know he can do that, too.

Nobody says anything for a while. We listen to Silver gobbling up his food and watch Mrs Boudry bustling about the kitchen. When she opens the oven, the most delicious smell fills the air. Willow gasps and Mrs B laughs.

"I expect you're hungry after climbing trees all morning."

Piper's mouth falls open and she stares at Willow in shock. "How does she know?" she mouths.

I can't help laughing even though I have a mouthful of fizz; it nearly comes out of my nose. I kick Jack under the table so that he'll answer Mrs Boudry.

"Ow! Um - yeah, we are really hungry. How did you know we'd been climbing trees?"

I roll my eyes and point at Piper. "Maybe because Piper's covered in green stains and she's got leaves stuck in her hair. And *you've* got apple blossom on your head." I laugh.

Mrs Boudry laughs too. Her face is round and pink and cheerful. She pulls out an enormous tray of biscuits and scones and tips them onto a cooling rack, and then she fetches plates down from a big shelf.

"Here, then," she says. "You'll have to wait until they cool down." A minute later, she puts two scones on each plate and starts placing the biscuits in a little tin. "Right, then. You can eat these now and take those up with you."

We are each passed a plate of fresh scones and Mrs Boudry even splits mine open for me with a knife. She puts a butter dish in the middle of the table and Willow jumps up to get some more knives. Mrs B then puts the tin of biscuits on the table, leaning the lid against the lemonade bottle to let the heat rise off the biscuits. I study it through the steam of my scone. The tin is red, and the lid has a picture of a ship on it. The ship has big white sails and it's sailing on a bright blue sea, beside a desert island with golden sand and bright green palm trees. All around the sides of the tin are small pictures - black footprints wandering up and down. I turn the tin around but the footsteps just keep going. I pick up my knife and dip it in the butter.

"Cheese and onion!" Willow says, her cheeks bulging with scone. Aunt Seren would definitely tell her off for speaking with such a big mouthful of food. "These are so yummy, Mrs Boudry, thank you!"

Mrs Boudry smiles. "You enjoy them, dear," she says. "Now I've got jobs to be getting on with." She goes to the sink and starts clattering dishes, but the clattering gets quieter and quieter, and Mrs B gets more and more see-through until, as we watch in amazement, she completely disappears.

"I LOVE it here," says Jack.

Piper's Lucky Coin

Willow

I'm trying not to laugh at Piper, because on the surface she has her sensible, trying-to-be-a-grown-up face on, but underneath I know she is full of the same enormous excitement bubbles that we are. So her face is making all sorts of peculiar expressions while she tries to decide which person she's going to be. Also, Silver has stolen the hair bobble she left on the chair - we've discovered he loves chewy elastic-y things - and she hasn't noticed yet, which is making me giggle. I'm sure Silver has a bit of a guilty look on his face, even while the bobble is hanging out the side of his mouth. Piper's standing in the middle of Headquarters staring at nothing, trying to re-plait her hair. It's grown loads and now it's past her shoulders. It's the same colour as mine, but hers is straight where mine is wavy - more like our mum's and Aunt Seren's.

Jack and Kit are leaning over the table looking at the scrapbook. They're trying to decide how to get to the top of the house without going up the main stairs, which takes us too close to the Office Wing. I'm sitting watching them, marvelling at the magical book. When we got back to Headquarters there was nothing new on the picture, but Kit turned the page and there's a sketch of the front of the house, with a tiny flag sticking out of the attic room window, and the three little parrots circling above it. It feels like that pause before you do something exciting, like waiting in the queue for a rollercoaster, or sitting in the cinema before the film starts. Like the room is holding its breath. Now that we're not hungry or thirsty any more there's nothing stopping us from beginning our search

- except for the minor fact that we don't have a clue where we're going. What if we get lost? It ought to be impossible to get lost in your own home, but Merryshields is so enormous *anything* seems possible.

I can still taste the cheesy onion from the scones. The biscuit tin is safely in my bag so we have something to snack on later. Piper has finally noticed the missing bobble and is huffing about it.

"Silver?" she says suspiciously. She's trying to be cross, but when Silver trots over and deposits the soggy bobble at her feet she can't help smiling at him. "It's a good job you're so cute," she tells him, sighing in exasperation but scratching his ears all the same.

"What do you think, girls?" Jack asks. Piper comes over. The drawing doesn't help a lot, to be honest, but Kit is looking cheerful, so Piper and I exchange glances and decide to be positive.

"Um, well, I suppose we have to decide which stairs to take," Piper says, sliding her finger next to the little Headquarters window.

"Not the main ones," Kit says immediately. "The Olds might see us, and we don't want questions. But there's that dark set of stairs, if we turn left, or that smelly set of stairs if we turn right."

"Yes," Jack agrees. "So when we go out of the corridor, should we turn left or right?"

Kit says, "Left," at the same time I say, "Right."

"Let's not waste time arguing about it," Piper interrupts. "I've got a coin in my pocket. Let's flip it."

Jack raises his eyebrows. "Why have you got a coin in your pocket? It's not as though we're going to go anywhere to spend it for, like, *months*."

Piper scowls. "If you must know, it's my lucky holiday coin. I've been carrying it around since we're not going on holidays any time soon."

"Why is it lucky?" Kit asks. Piper looks at me again, and now I can see the sadness behind her scowl.

"Remember when we went to Tenerife last year, with Mum and Dad?" she says. I suddenly know what she's going to say and I move a bit closer to her. "Well, we were having a really horrible day - do you remember, Will? It had rained all week and Mum and Dad were arguing and we were cooped up in the hotel loads, and both of us had tummy upsets... anyway, it stopped raining that afternoon and we went down to the beach and I found a coin in the sand. And after that - well, everything seemed better. We went for a meal and me and Willow felt better and we ate a massive pizza, and Mum and Dad shared an ice cream and we thought everything was going to be alright... Well, anyway, it just felt like... like the coin was lucky. That's all."

Silver nudges her leg and she looks down at him, and Jack and Kit look at each other and then at me.

"I think it is a lucky coin," Kit says. "And this is a lucky house, so it's double luck."

I lean closer to her and nudge her shoulder with mine. "I think that too," I say. "Go on, Pi, flip it."

She flashes me a quick, small smile and pulls the coin out of her pocket. "Alright," she says. "Heads we turn right, tails we turn left."

She flicks the coin with her thumb. We watch it spin through the air and land flat on the table right over the spot where Kit has drawn a little flag.

Jack cocks his head to one side. "So it's a foreign coin?"

Piper nods. "Ye-es... but it didn't have that on it before."

I lean closer. Instead of an unrecognisable monarch, the coin is engraved with a wooden chest, treasure spilling out over the top of it. It's exactly like those pretend pirate coins you get, but this one is definitely *real*. It's gold, though it looks grimy and old, as though it has travelled all over the world and passed through the hands of hundreds of sailors.

Piper picks it up and weighs it in the palm of her hand. "It's heavier," she whispers disbelievingly.

"So does that count as heads or tails?" Kit asks.

Piper turns it over. On the other side of the coin is a bearded man with an eyepatch, glowering straight out at us - heads. She quickly turns it back to the treasure. "Left it is, then."

Kit does a little excited hop as we leave Headquarters and walk down the corridor. "I wonder if that's the treasure we'll find when we get there."

"Why do you think we'll find treasure?" I ask him.

Jack and Kit look at each other. They have obviously been talking about this.

"Well," says Jack carefully, "we think the house gives us whatever we need. I mean, we needed to eat and Mrs Boudry appeared; we needed fruit, so the trees grew some..."

"And I needed a dog!" Kit adds.

Silver looks up at him and barks. His nails are clitter-clattering noisily along the floor. Piper and I share a look, seeing several flaws in this argument.

"But," I start, "we didn't *need* a key, and that just appeared. We didn't *need* the birds, either."

Piper interrupts me at this. "Have any of you seen the birds since?"

Kit bounces again, his hand in the air. "I have!" he cries. He can barely contain his excitement. "I saw them this morning. I put my head around the door to see if they were still there. I didn't let Silver in, though."

"Why not?" says Jack.

Kit looks at his brother in surprise. "Beee-cause," he says slowly, as if stating the obvious, "I don't want the room to take him back."

We all stop walking and look at each other. This hasn't occurred to me before, but now that Kit has mentioned it, it does seem worryingly possible.

"Do you think that could happen?" I ask.

Piper is frowning in concern, looking down at Silver. "I don't know," she says. "I mean, it's not like we've got any idea *how* he came to be alive, is it? If it's something to do with that room..."

"We definitely can't risk going back," Jack says firmly, nodding at Kit.

Kit nods back, and we all look at the dog, who is sitting and scratching his ear with his hind leg. He looks up at us, tongue flopping out one side of his mouth.

"Yep," Piper says. "That door's staying firmly shut from now on."

We start walking again. I feel relieved, as though I've avoided a risk I didn't know we were taking.

"So," I say, "to go back to the house... *Technically,* we didn't need the fruit either. I mean, it was nice, but it's not like we were actually starving."

"Well, we definitely need treasure." Piper glances at me and gestures toward the house around her. I think of Mum. Of Aunt Seren and Uncle Peter working so hard in the Office Wing. Even of Great-Aunt Glynis. I nod back at her decidedly.

"Then the adults could do whatever they need to do, *and* maybe we could go on holiday - when we're allowed to go out into the world again." Piper's tone is brisk now, as if she's shrugged off all the sad thoughts. "Now, should we turn down that corridor or through that door?"

She points around the corner towards the East Wing with one hand, and to a small, narrow door with the other. It looks like the most ordinary door in the world, but there is something inviting about it - perhaps it's the gleam of light on the handle, or the way the knots in the wood sort of make a smiley face.

We consider for a moment. The air is very still and we can't hear a sound from anywhere.

"It's like the door that leads to the kitchen corridor," Jack says, examining it. "Narrow, I mean. Not like the wide doorways to the rooms."

He puts his hand on the door handle, but Kit suddenly grabs him, and we all jump. It's getting to be quite a regular occurrence, the jumping.

Kit's voice is hushed and worried. "If we *do* find treasure and we give it to the Olds, then what if they start asking where it came from, or following us around? Or what if they start doing stuff to the house that changes it, and it's not magic any more?"

We take a minute to digest this troubling thought.

Piper is the one to break the silence first. "But we can't just let them be stressed out and miserable all the time, Kit. Not if we can help them."

"What if we find treasure but they can't see it, like they can't see Silver?" I ask. "It'll be useless!"

Jack shakes his head. "Let's just see if there *is* any treasure, first. Then we can decide what to do next."

This seems sensible. After all, it's unlikely that we're going to stop living in the house any time soon, and as long as we don't get into trouble while we're searching, everything should be fine.

Kit breathes a sigh of relief and turns the handle. "Good idea!" He darts through the open doorway ahead of Jack.

The Room Behind the Door

Jack

The door opens onto a flight of stairs, which are narrow and dark after the wide, light corridor. It gets darker when the door closes behind us. The girls gasp. I don't blame them. Me and Kit have already seen this particularly amazing thing so we aren't as shocked as they are, but I have to admit, it's still pretty cool.

"Kit!" Piper says. "Look at Silver!"

"I know!" Kit says. "He does that sometimes." Kit is racing up the stairs ahead of us and is panting. (I told him last night that he could be the scout on our missions, searching ahead for danger. He liked that idea.)

"But... he's glowing!" Piper says, her eyes wide. She does state the obvious sometimes.

"But not like glow-in-the-dark," Willow says, hurrying to catch up. "He's lit up silvery, like a star."

We - me and my brother - had noticed it at bedtime on Silver's first night. (Well, his *second* night, if you count the fact that I couldn't see Silver on the first.) Kit and I share a room here. Seemed stupid at first when the house is so big, but I like having all the crew within reach. Kit chatters in his sleep and I can hear the girls in their room just across the corridor. Piper talks, too, and Willow always holds on to something. Silver jumped up onto Kit's bed to sleep and when we turned the light off, he was shining - just gently. Willow was right when she said it's not a glow-in-the-dark kind of glow, but I think the way it works might be sort of the same. My theory is, Silver soaks up all the sunlight when he's running round during the day, and then whenever it's dark he glows silver, like the moon. There must be some scientific reason for it. My dad says that magic is just science we don't know yet, so I think Silver is the exact mixture of magic and science that he means.

Up two flights of stairs, Kit looks at me and I nod so he carries on up the next. It's hot and stuffy up here. We're all out of breath by the time we get to the top. Kit opens another door and then hangs back, looking wary. A second later, the girls and I can see why.

Well, I mean we can *smell* why.

"Is that... fish?" Willow asks. She wrinkles her nose in disgust.

Piper sniffs and leans forward cautiously. Her face is very red and shiny and when she catches my eye, she puffs defensively. "Well, was there any particular reason we had to *sprint* up the stairs?"

I shrug. "I just wanted to keep up with Kit," I say. My heart is pounding, but I make myself look cool and relaxed.

"It is fish," Willow says over our bickering. "But it's smoky. Like it's being cooked on a..."

"Barbecue!" Kit says.

"Yeah! Or a fire on a beach," Willow says, nodding.

She's right. It smells like seaweed after a hot day. A smoky, fresh fish smell. Then there's a salty gust of wind that blows all our hair out of our faces. It gets up Silver's nose too and makes him bark.

"Oh my goodness," Piper says. She's gone from red to pale.

"Come on," I say. It's clear they need a leader in this expedition. The smell of fish had momentarily distracted me, but now it's time to resume our mission. "Let's go."

It's so strange. Everything looks exactly the same. This corridor is narrower than the ones downstairs, but it still looks like the same house. The same creaky floorboards, the same plain walls, the same scuffed skirting boards. There are doors all along both sides of this corridor and most of them are closed. The few that are open let in a bit of light from the windows, and I try not to get distracted by peering into them as we pass.

"It must be all the way to the end," Willow whispers.

"I think so," I say. "Is it me, or is it quite warm up here?"

"We have just been running," Piper says, but she meets my eye and nods.

I stop and close my eyes, ignoring the others bumping into me. It's easy to think that the house is just the house when you're looking at it, but with my eyes closed, it *feels* exactly like being by the coast. Even...

"Did you hear that?" I ask. Everyone is behind me, looking nervous.

"Hear what?" Piper snaps. She is not coping well with all of these unusual things. I have a feeling she is in for a *long* day.

Silver's head has snapped up and his ears are alert. He lets out a short, sharp bark, as though he's heard something very interesting, and looks at Kit expectantly. The noise comes again.

"Seagulls!" I say.

"That's impossible!" Piper says.

We all look at her and then burst out laughing. Even she has a bit of a giggle.

"Let's keep going," Willow says.

I clap her on the shoulder. "Aye aye, matey," I say. "On-wards!" I point ahead and grin back at Piper, who smiles at me with a determined look on her face. Kit nudges my elbow to show he understands - usually it's just me and Kit who sail the ship on our imaginary voyages, but now the girls are part of the crew, too. Today we're all on board together.

Kit races down the corridor ahead of us, Silver flapping at his heels, and we run after him. The nearer we get to the end of the corridor, the louder the sound of the sea becomes, until finally we reach a corner. I look down it and then reverse a bit, to the last-but-one open door.

"Look," I whisper to the others, pointing out of the window. "We're definitely at the front of the house, and we can see where the orchard is."

"Which means," Willow says, turning around so her back is to the window and closing her eyes, "if *this* is us, in the trees," she wiggles one hand, "then the flag was..." she wiggles the other hand high in the air, "here."

"Here," Piper says, looking around us. "We must be in the right place."

"And it was the very last window in that row," Kit says.

"Yep," Piper agrees. "At the very top."

We all automatically look up at the ceiling. We can't get any higher without going on the roof.

We all walk back to the end of the corridor again and look at the last door. It looks very ordinary.

"Right," I say, although I can feel the nerves swishing in my tummy. "Let's go in."

I open the door.

We all gasp.

Instead of a room, we're looking at a long stretch of white sand that curves away and dips out of sight. To the left, the sea laps against the shore. In the distance, the sea is darker, breaking over a reef with foamy white waves. White clouds skid across the blue sky. Palm trees tower to our right, waving in the breeze, and beyond them is a dense thicket of jungle that grows as far as I can see. Just visible beside a pile of dark boulders at the edge of the jungle, a fire burns with a broad log beside it, like a bench. A big old wooden barrel has a knife lying on it, glinting in the sun. Three fish lie on a slab of rock, gently smoking, and above them, three red parrots sit close together, on a tree branch that's bobbing in the wind.

I close the door with a snap.

"Did we just see that?" I ask, even though I can still feel sand where it's blown against my legs.

They all nod.

Piper walks back along the corridor a little way and opens the door to the room next to this one.

"Empty," she says. "Completely normal." Her voice sounds funny.

I take a deep breath. The nerves are turning into bubbles of excitement.

"Well," I say, "what are we waiting for? Let's go to the sea-side!"

I open the door again, and go in.

Castaways

Piper

I think we're going to stay here forever.

The minute we step over the threshold, I feel the heat of the sun. I have a mad urge to run downstairs for the suncream and I almost laugh. Jack walks straight into the middle of the beach and stands with his hands on his hips, surveying the surroundings. Kit and Silver both immediately run into the sea. Silver is jumping and splashing, and Kit's squealing; they are absolutely soaked within seconds. I don't think it'll matter too much. It's so hot they'll dry in minutes.

I take my trainers off and put them together neatly on the sand. I don't know why I do it, really. They look a bit ridiculous. Willow is standing behind me, so I pick them up again and try to hand them to her.

"Hey, Willow, put these against the door so--"

But it's too late. As Willow looks at me, she takes a step forward and lets go of the door.

Bang! It disappears.

"Willow!" I shriek. "What have you done?!"

Willow looks absolutely horrified. "Piper!" she cries. "What...? How-how was I to know it would disappear? Oh no, oh no..."

Jack turns around at the noise and comes striding across the sand towards us.

"Where's the door?" he demands.

I glare at Willow. I feel sick to my stomach. I turn around, slowly, looking at the expanse of empty sand and the thick, threatening tangle of undergrowth that could be harbouring any number of man-eating monsters just waiting to devour four tasty children. How on earth was I supposed to keep them all safe? *How were going to get home?*

"Piper was talking to me--" Willow begins.

"Don't blame me!" I flared. "*You* were the one who let go of the door!"

We all stare at the place where the door had been. The sand unfolds in front of us; nothing but turquoise sea on one side and jungle on the other.

"Right," I say, a little wildly. "Willow, leave your shoes here, too. We'll walk along the beach. Maybe there's another door to a different room in the house. Then, if we don't find anything, we'll turn back and walk the other way."

"Maybe me and Kit should walk the other way to save time," Jack suggests, but I shriek before he can close his mouth.

"Are you stupid?! Anything could happen! No matter what, we have to stay together!" I angrily plonk my trainers down where the door *should* have been, and start to walk, my heart racing in terror. The gorgeous scenery now feels menacing. Realising nobody is following me, I turn around and lift my hand to shade my eyes so that I can see.

Kit and Silver have finally realised that something has happened. They emerge from the water, still dripping. Kit squints up and down the beach, and then joins Jack and Willow. The three of them draw closer together and begin to talk earnestly. I close my eyes. I'm glad I can't hear them. After a few seconds, they join me.

Nobody says a word.

We walk for ages and ages, around the curve of the beach, all of us getting more and more scared. The sun beats down, and the sea rushes in and out relentlessly. Kit's hand is resting on Silver's back as they walk side-by-side, and Willow is so close to my side she keeps bumping into me.

"Stop it," I say crossly. "It's bad enough without you barging into me all the time."

Willow's face crumples in on itself. She looks so sad I almost feel sorry for her until I remember she was the one who got us into this mess.

I avoid her eyes and keep my gaze fixed on the horizon, constantly scanning for a secret door to let us through. My lips are dry and my tummy is grumbling. Even the soft sand under my feet, which usually would make me feel delighted, is just making my calves ache.

"We've been walking for *hours*," Kit groans. His voice is tiny.

"Not hours," Jack says, looking at his watch. "Nearly one whole hour, though." He glances at me and I can see he's wondering if we should turn back and go the other way. We surely would have seen something by now if there was going to be another door. I nod.

Without warning, Silver jumps away from Kit's hand and gallops off down the beach, his silly long tail wagging.

"Where's he going?" Jack asks, as Kit runs after him.

"He's seen something!" Kit calls back over his shoulder.

We hurry after them, and within minutes we see Silver turn around and come back to Kit, bouncing joyfully. Something is hanging from his mouth.

"What's he got?" Jack asks.

"That's my *shoe*!" I say. "I don't *believe* it! Silver, drop that!"

He doesn't listen to me, but barks playfully with his mouth full and darts away again. I sprint after him, my eyes fixed on a point beyond Kit and Silver. As I get closer, I can see Willow's shoes and my one remaining trainer are still sitting neatly in a line. I stop beside them, relieved to see them still there, and wipe sweat off my face as I wait for the others to catch up.

"You know what this means," Willow says.

I nod, my heart beating erratically,

"We've walked in a circle," Kit breathes. His eyes are enormous and panicked.

"We're on an island," Jack says slowly.

"We're *stuck* on an island, you mean!" My voice sounds hysterical, and I don't even try to stop it. "How on earth are we going to get home?! We don't even know where we are!"

"Technically, we're still <u>at</u> home," Willow says shakily. "But obviously it's not ideal," she adds quickly, seeing my face.

I turn my back on them all and walk quickly away across the sand to the shelter of a palm tree. I cannot believe Willow was stupid enough to let go of our only way back into the house. She's walking in a circle around the spot where the door had been, staring intently down at the sand. I roll my eyes. It isn't as though the door is going to suddenly spring back into existence again.

If I close my eyes, it's easy to imagine that we're just on holiday. The sound of the waves shushing in and out is relaxing, and so is the sound of the wind rustling through the towering palm trees. There might even be coconuts, I think idly. And maybe somewhere in the undergrowth we might find pineapples. I lean back against the nearest tree trunk. I'm sitting on short, rough grass, but there's sand beneath my toes and I wiggle them, trying not to let the panic rise. Willow's right. We are still *technically* in the house, and there is bound to be a way back somewhere on this island. We just have to find it. Perhaps I had shouted at her unfairly. After all, anyone might have let go of the door. I do wish we'd brought that scrapbook, though. The house might have shown us a way off the island - or out of the room, depending on how you look at it. This would be the ideal time for a map. In fact, I think right now I would swap a treasure map for an escape map.

I take a deep breath in, thinking about all the pictures on the first page of the map, and then breathe out. There was a palm tree on the map, I think idly. Maybe Jack and Kit are right about there being treasure somewhere in Merryshields. You'd think a desert island would be the best place to find it. I can taste salt on my lips and I have a sudden memory of fish and chips from the last time we went to the beach. I breathe in again and smell fish. My eyes snap open and I sit bolt upright with a horrible jolt of realisation.

"You guys!" I hiss, sprinting back down the beach towards them. "You guys! We can't stay here!"

Jack indicates the lack-of-door. "Looks like we don't have a choice," he says.

"That's not what I mean!" I look around urgently, feeling suddenly and desperately exposed. "Come on, *please*!" I grab Kit's arm and drag him back up the beach to where the undergrowth looks thickest. "Remember the pirate?!" I say pointedly, staring at them all as I stumble backwards over the sand.

I see the realisation cross Willow's face. Jack's eyes flick up to the campsite and the slab of rock where we saw the fish.

It's empty. The fish have gone. And so have the parrots. I meet Jack's eyes and nod.

"Yep!" I say. "We're trapped on a desert island with a pirate!"

As one, we all turn and run as fast as we can back up the beach, ducking in and out of the line of palm trees, hoping against hope that we haven't been seen.

Scouting

Kit

I f you'd told me a week ago that I was going to get trapped on a desert island with a pirate, I would have laughed - nothing that cool ever happens to anyone, not in real life. But, number one: all kinds of cool things happen in this house. And number two: it isn't turning out to be as much fun as I thought it would be.

After creeping through countless tiny spaces between the enormous bushes, which all grow so close together you can barely see the ground, we finally stop and squish together in a place the size of my mam's bed - which isn't very big when there are four of us and one wriggly dog, all trying to stay quiet and get comfy.

"We have to go further into the jungle," Jack says. He is using what Dad calls his 'intense eyes'. It's what his face looks like when he is completely, totally serious, and it makes me feel scared.

"We *can't*," Piper argues. "We don't know where this person is, and it's a lot easier for one person to hear all of us coming."

"If it *is* just one person," Willow says. She's looked sick ever since the door disappeared, but now she looks like she might actually throw up. "There might be more."

"We should stay here, stay quiet, and watch," Piper says. She looks pale but her voice is firm. She doesn't look at me but puts her arm out and I lean in, and Silver puts his head on my knee. Willow nods, and Jack sighs.

"Fine," he says, lifting his hands in defeat. "But we can't sit here indefinitely. We'll take it in turns to go and watch - the campsite <u>and</u> the beach. Then we can see what's going on and make the next decision."

He goes off, sneaking silently, and we all settle down uncomfortably, and listen to the sounds of the jungle around us.

He's gone for ages, long enough for me to start worrying, but comes back looking serious, shaking his head. Piper moves away wordlessly and then, when she comes back, so does Willow. Then Jack again, and so it goes on for ages. I fidget. The branches are spiky and the leaves are big, and they keep slapping my shoulders every time the wind blows (which is all the time). There is a plant next to me that is MASSIVE. The leaves look thick and fleshy, like they would get hurt if they were spiked. I stroke it, carefully, just in case it likes it. We are still in the house, after all, and I remember Piper's tree in the orchard that liked it when she told it that it was the best. There are bright flowers everywhere, all pinks and reds and oranges. It smells a bit like a holiday, but without the suncream. Mam would definitely make us wear suncream.

My shorts have dried from being in the sea, and now they're all hard. Piper says it's because of the salty water. She's calmed down now. I'm glad Willow packed that tin of biscuits in her bag. We ate them ages ago, even though Piper said we ought to save them, but we're still hungry and now we're thirsty, too. Jack has come back again from his fourth patrol of the area.

"We *need* to find a way off this island," he says, wetting his finger and dabbing up all the crumbs from the bottom of the biscuit tin.

Piper rolls her eyes. "What do you think we've been doing?"

"*Not* looking for a way off the island?" Jack snaps.

I sort of agree but I don't say anything, because I'm worried Piper's head will explode. I do wonder what we're going to do, though.

"Why don't I go actually *onto* the beach and see if the door reappears?" Willow says. She gets to her feet. "It might be, like, a time thing? Where it pops back after a certain number of hours?"

Piper grabs her arm and pulls her back down into the bushes. "No! You can't go into the open!"

"Who's turn is it, anyway?" Jack sighs.

"I think it's mine," I say. I gently move Silver off my leg and brush the sand off my shorts.

At first, none of the others want to let me have a turn of keeping watch, but that's just ridiculous. I'm as good at watching as anyone. How hard can it be? You're literally just... watching...

I say, "If you don't let me, I'm going to jump up and down and yell and make loads of noise." I bend my knees in readiness to show I mean it.

Jack looks furious.

"I'll break your arms if you even *move*," he says.

I know he's really worried because he doesn't usually say stuff like that unless I've really, really wound him up. So I stop still, but I look him right in his eyes and say - quietly, but so he knows I mean it - "JUST BECAUSE I AM THE YOUNGEST CREWMATE DOESN'T MEAN I CAN'T DO ANYTHING."

His face stops being furious, though his mouth is still in a very straight line.

I say, "You always let me be the scout at home." And I keep my eyes looking straight into his eyes.

There's not much he can say now. Because if he says, 'Yes, but that's at home,' then that means we're *not* at home, and this game is *not* a game, and everything that's happening now is *real*. And I don't want to think about it being real. That's too scary. I want it to stay being a game. And I want my brother to make it alright.

Jack nods slowly, and I know he understands.

"Alright, shipmate, you know what to do."

I squeeze through the gap in the bushes. Behind me, the girls start whispering to Jack that he shouldn't have let me go, but Jack tells them to shut up and that I know what I'm doing.

Sometimes I love my brother.

I wriggle along the narrow track until I get to the spot where I can see the pirate's campsite. It looks exactly the same. The fire is much smaller, but otherwise nothing has changed. I wriggle a bit further, going around the campsite until I can see the beach, and I gasp. My heart starts racing like a hundred horses. Out at sea, a ship is floating. It doesn't seem to be moving, just rocking back and forth, but I can see moment on the deck and a tiny glint, as though someone is holding a telescope.

I hurry back to the squished patch to tell the others. They all stop talking as soon as I get there and look down at the ground.

"What?" I ask.

"Nothing," Piper says. She's trying to look innocent, but I know her. She is twiddling with one of her plaits and has forgotten to relax her eyebrows - they're raised right up to her forehead.

I raise my own eyebrows right back at her.

"It's nothing," Jack says to me. I turn to him and scan his face, eyes narrowed. "I promise," he says. He sticks out his hands and puts the fingers in-between each other, so they make a cross. We call it the Cross of Truth. I let my eyebrows down but keep looking at him, and he shakes the Cross of Truth at me again. "Honestly," he says. "The girls just didn't want you to know that they're worried.

Piper and Willow are shocked when he says this and give him furious looks that say SHUT UP, but it makes sense to me. They've forgotten what it's like when you're eight. People - mostly adults - don't realise how much you understand, so they talk about things in what they *think* is code. They think you won't realise that they're worrying about something, as though you can't tell that they're worried without them saying WE ARE WORRIED right in your face.

"I'm worried too," I tell them, in what I hope is a reassuring voice. "But we'll think of something, won't we?"

They don't say anything for a while, and then Willow says sadly, "I hope so." She's feeling guilty because she thinks it's all her fault. (Which it sort of is. But there's no need for us to rub it in.)

"Well, if you hadn't let go of the door," Piper says, and then she quickly says, "Joking!" But it's too late. Willow starts to cry. Piper puts her arm around her and says, "Sorry, Willow, I didn't mean it," and Jack looks away because he hates it when anyone gets upset and he can't make it better with a funny joke. Then Silver's tummy rumbles so loudly that even he looks surprised by it, and everyone laughs a bit and sniffs a bit.

And then we sit and think about what on earth we're going to do next.

Camping Beneath The Stars

Willow

I t's getting dark really quickly. (Luckily, I have Jack's torch in my bag and he's too het up about being stuck here to argue about me using it.) I can't believe it's all my fault that we're stuck here in the middle of the ocean--and we don't even know which ocean! Merryshields is so close but impossible to reach.

We still haven't seen the pirate and the ship hasn't moved either; it's just bobbing there, no closer but no farther away. Piper and Jack had a small but intense argument about whether or not it belongs to the pirate--Piper says it must, and Jack says it could just be a coincidence--but thankfully, they seem to have called a truce.

It's a lot noisier than I thought it would be on an island at night. The warm wind is streaming through the trees over our heads, and there are dozens of birds fluttering and squawking as night settles in. Leaves brush against each other, sounding a bit like the sea, and every other second, I'm sure I can hear footsteps shuffling across the sand. We're sitting on a squashed pile of leaves and branches that aren't very comfortable, but we're afraid to move around too much and draw attention to ourselves.

Silver's tummy is rumbling--and his is not the only one. There's still a faint smell of fish in the air, beneath the salty sea scent, and Jack suggests we steal the food from the pirate's fire. Piper and I stop that idea in its tracks, though. The last thing we want to do is make him angry. And as Piper points out, we don't even know what sort of fish it is. It could make us sick.

"It's not like Mrs Boudry's cooking it, Jack," Piper hisses at him.

Jack stands up, looking like he wants to argue. He gets really irritable when he's hungry.

"At the moment, the pirate doesn't know we're here," I say quickly, before he can say anything. "If we steal his food, he'll definitely know."

Thankfully, Jack sees the sense in this and sits down again.

Piper looks up into the trees overhead. "The birds have gone quiet."

She's right. The wind has dropped, too, so the sound of the waves on the shore seems louder than it did before.

"Do you think the tide will come all the way up here?" Jack asks.

I feel a brief flash of panic, but shake my head straight away. "No, definitely not. Otherwise, all these plants wouldn't be here, would they?"

We fall silent again. After a while, someone has to state the obvious, so Piper clears her throat.

"I think we should all try and make ourselves as comfy as possible," she says. There's a little catch in her voice, but I'm the only one who notices it. "We're not going to find our way home now. It's too dark. We may as well accept it and get as much rest as we can, and hopefully when the sun comes up the door will have reappeared. You never know."

We all sigh.

"I don't want to stay here all night. I'm hungry." Kit's voice is very small.

Jack puts his arm around him. "Me too. But think how many stars we might see! We've never stayed on a desert island before."

"We've never done anything on a desert island before," I mutter.

We all try to lie down without making too much noise, and watch as the sky grows darker and darker, the blue turning to navy and, eventually, to black. Jack is right about the stars. There are more of them than I have ever seen in my whole life! The sky is full of them, spread out thickly, as far as we could see. They're absolutely incredible.

But it goes without saying that they don't make the ground any more comfortable. In fact, it's the most uncomfortable night I've ever had in my life--and that's including that time we went camping and forgot the mattresses, and the time I had chicken pox and every bit of me was itchy (including my hair)! We start off snuggled together, but then one person needs to move, or another person's leg goes to sleep because someone is leaning on it, or an elbow is poking into a rib, or a foot in a face, and then Piper mutters in her sleep and Jack twitches in his, and Silver keeps getting up and turning around, nosing each of us in the face every time he does to make sure we are all still here. So what with that and the dark, and the unusual noises, and the fact that we're waiting for the pirate to discover us at any second, I for one am extremely relieved when the sky gets paler again. The stars fade, the sky above the ocean goes pink, then orange, and then gold, and the birds start to sing.

We all struggle into sitting positions, rubbing our faces and yawning. Jack's hair is flat on one side and Piper's face is haloed by fuzzy flyaway hairs. Apart from being pale and crumpled, everyone looks pretty normal, although all of our tummies are complaining like mad.

Kit is the first to speak. "Should we go and explore the inside of the island? There might be another door somewhere?"

I think about this. After all, two doors on a deserted island is as likely-- or unlikely--as one was. I am just about to agree when Silver makes a low, grumbling sound, deep down in his throat.

"He's growling," Kit whispers. He puts his hand on Silver's collar, but even I can see that Silver's attention is completely focused on something that we can't hear.

Jack gets up and starts to creep away, fingers on his lips to tell us to be quiet. "I'll go to the lookout point," he mouths.

We wait anxiously. Silver continues to grumble. When Jack's face pops back through the bushes, we all jump. He looks white.

"The pirate's back!"

It's like we're the same person, because we all gasp at the exact same time.

"He's sleeping in the hammock," Jack gestures back the way he came. "Those three red parrots are there, too. All in a line. The fish has gone. And--" he pauses to take a breath, as if gathering courage, "--there's a rowing boat coming from the pirate ship with three more pirates inside!"

"What do we do?!" Piper is immediately in panic-mode.

A sudden squawk above our heads makes us jump again. There, soaring in a circle over our tiny clearing, is one of the scarlet parrots. Silver goes completely bananas. He barks and leaps around, totally ignoring Kit who is trying desperately to calm him down, even though it's clearly too late for us to stay hidden. The two of them tussle further and further away from us through the bushes. Then, without warning, Silver darts through the undergrowth in the direction of the campsite.

"SILVER!" Kit bellows after him. "Come back!"

Before we can stop him, Kit sprints after his dog, yelling and calling his name. A split-second's shocked pause and we all tear after him, galumphing like elephants through the jungle.

Somewhere ahead I hear Silver bark once, and then an unfamiliar deep voice shouting, "OHO THERE!". My heart stops completely and then starts again twice as fast.

"KIT!" Jack cries, picking up his pace.

We burst through the trees and find ourselves in the middle of the campsite. The hammock is swinging, empty. The ash from the fire is scattered all over the sand. Of Kit, Silver and the pirate, there is no sign at all.

A Lost Brother

Jack

I've lost Kit.

This is the worst thing that's ever happened to me. How on earth am I going to explain this to mam and dad? Maybe I'll never have to explain it to them, since we seem to be stuck on this stupid island. Even if we can get back, I'm not going without my brother. He might be stupid sometimes, but he's MY stupid.

I can't believe he's gone.

We stand in the pirate's ruined campsite for a few minutes, all of us out of breath and panting noisily. It looks like there's been some kind of fight. My tummy goes all twisty with worry and my heart is pounding so loudly I think everyone can hear it. There are fish bones everywhere and bits of charcoal from the fire. But there is no noise at all, apart from the sea. From here, I can't see the rowing boat that Kit told us about, but it must be getting closer which means we are running out of time.

"This is ridiculous," Piper says, whirling around. "Where could they have gone? They can't just vanish!"

"The door did," Willow says. She looks like she might be sick. I feel a bit like that too, but after not eating anything for hours I don't think it's very likely. I swallow uncomfortably.

"That makes sense, though," I say. My voice sounds funny and tight. "The door disappearing, I mean. It obviously only existed because it was open. But *people* don't just vanish for no reason."

"Then where are they?" Piper demands.

A huge bubble of anger builds up inside me and bursts. "I don't know!" I yell. "Do you think I would just be standing here if I did?!"

Tears well up in Willow's eyes. "Don't fight," she pleads. "It won't make anything better. They have to be here some-where." She rubs her face with both hands and takes a huge, shaky breath. "Right," she says, through her fingers. "Let's think."

"I *am* thinking," Piper growls.

Willow sighs. "I'll go and get my bag," she says. "Then at least we've got our things with us."

"I wish you'd put a drink in your bag," I say, not for the first time.

"I will every time after this," she replies.

"There won't be any more times," Piper says grimly. "We're going to be grounded forever."

"They can't ground us from the house," I say.

Piper glares at me. "They can if we've lost Kit!" she says. Her voice is shrill and high pitched and she looks like she's going to cry.

Willow flaps her arms at us both. "Just shut up a minute, both of you! I've just thought--when we got here, to the camp-site, we couldn't hear them rushing through all the bushes and undergrowth, could we?"

We shake our heads.

"So it's obvious," Willow says. "They must have gone to the beach."

Piper and I turn as one and rush to the narrow opening leading to the beach. The sand is completely empty. It's serene and peaceful. We look back at Willow, who's rolling her eyes.

"No, you idiots, they're obviously not there now. Look." She points. "The beach goes round that corner and disappears. We came straight into the campsite--we didn't even think to check the beach!"

Now she's said it, it's obvious that's where they must have gone. The anger bubbles again, but this time it's at myself for not thinking of it straight away. I turn around and kick the nearest tree, really hard. A coconut thumps down, narrowly missing my head.

"That was lucky," Willow says. She's trying to smile, but it's a bit wobbly.

Piper ignores this. "You're right, Willow," she says, nodding. "That must be what happened."

"Yes," Willow says. The best thing about Willow is she never says 'I told you so'. "I'll run and get my bag, and you two make a start along the beach, see if we can find a track to follow. I'll catch you up."

The sun has risen properly and it's getting really hot, really quickly. Willow joins us after just a few minutes, her bag bumping against her. The sand burns the soles of our feet, and we have to keep dipping them into the water to cool off. It's so hot because the sun has been burning for hours without any clouds getting in the way. We're walking as fast as we can on soft sand, our eyes stinging from staring into the brightness for clues. I get thirstier and thirstier, until I can hardly think of anything except where to find a drink. Willow's arms are burnt and so's the back of Piper's neck, and I can feel my own skin going all tight, too. The pirate ship sits menacingly in the water, but there is no rowing boat to be seen. None of us say out loud what we're all wondering--that it might have gone back to the ship with Kit on board. We don't say anything at all.

Then I hear barking.

"That's Silver!" I cry. "It *must* be!"

"Look!" Willow says. She points to a gap in the trees where a track leads inland.

"Come on," Piper says, as we hear the bark again, and we all begin to run, refreshed by the sound. "That means they've definitely not vanished."

That thought sends a little wave of hope through me. I try not to think that it might be another dog, or that it might be

Silver without Kit. It's better to just keep running towards the sound.

We all breathe a sigh of relief as we enter the shade of the trees and start along the little path through the undergrowth.

I wave at a small brown pile beside the path. "Well, Silver's definitely been here."

"Ew." Piper wrinkles her nose.

"I never thought I'd be happy to see one of those," Willow says.

I for one am more happy than you can measure to see a dog poo curled up on the sand. It makes my heart feel lighter, until we come to another clearing. We all gasp. There are no humans or dogs, but the most extraordinary sight is hanging in front of our eyes--and, considering where we are, that's saying something.

An Island View

Piper

We burst out from all the dense undergrowth into a round grassy area. There's nothing on the ground except sand, no plants growing, and we can see right up to the blue sky. And hanging in the middle of this little magical space is... a...

WINDOW.

Of course, we know which window it must be, so we run straight to it to peer out. It's really bizarre. We're standing on a desert island in the middle of an unknown ocean, sandy grass beneath our feet and burning hot sun on our backs, but through the window we can see the overcast Northumbrian sky, the lawn at the front of Merryshields stretching away into the distance, and--if we lean out--the orchard from where we first saw the pirate's arm yesterday.

"THAT'S why Silver was running!" I shout. "It has to be!"

"What?" Jack says, and then breathes in deeply. "Oh."

The smell of roasting chicken is strong and delicious and coming straight through the window towards us. My tummy makes an enormous rumble.

"Silver must have been able to smell that miles away," Jack groans, wafting the wind towards his nose.

Willow sticks her arm through the window. "It's drizzling," she says. "This is so weird. And that roasting chicken! Oh, my tummy."

Jack walks around the window. When he gets to the other side, I start to laugh.

"Can you see me?" he asks.

"I can only see your legs!" I chuckle.

Willow giggles. She still has her arm out of the window and is waving it around. "Can you see me?" she asks, bending down at the same time to look beneath the window. "I can see your legs Jack, and--ooh," she looks up, "my arm just disappears! This is *weird*." She withdraws her arm and steps back. "What do you think it means?"

Jack comes back around and the three of us stand in a line looking at the window.

"Well, Kit and Silver can't have gone through it," I say, stepping forwards and peering out. The air moves against my face, cool and damp. Then I look down and my stomach drops. I'm suddenly staring down several storeys at the gravel driveway. I stand up again quickly and go back to the others.

"No," Willow agrees. "They wouldn't have gone through without us. If they'd come here, they would still be around somewhere." She looks around her, hopefully.

"Do you think," Jack says, frowning, "that the pirate would have been able to see us? When we were climbing trees in the orchard, I mean?"

This is a new thought. It feels creepy to think of someone watching us. I shiver.

But Willow shakes her head. "You can barely see the orchard from here," she says, pointing. "The only reason we could see his arm from where we were yesterday is because it was sticking out and so obviously <u>not</u> a part of the window. If the pirate had wanted our attention to bring us up here, he would have stayed there longer and waved his flag, wouldn't he?"

"Exactly. And if the pirate couldn't see us, he also couldn't have known we were coming," I say, and put my arm around Jack. "But what do we do now?"

"Maybe Kit didn't come this way at all," Willow says gloomily. "Maybe he went down a different path in the jungle, and we missed it. It's no good having a way out if we haven't got Kit."

We're contemplating this uncomfortable fact when we hear a shout coming from behind us.

"Jack! JACK!"

Jack moves as if he is lightning. "Kit!" he roars. "I'm coming! Where are you?" He is already racing back the way we came, and with a swift glance at each other, Willow and I follow.

It takes less than five seconds to see him. He bowls straight into Jack, nearly knocking him over as he throws his arms around him.

"Where were you?" Kit demands.

"Where were *you*?" I retort. The relief at seeing him has suddenly turned into fury. "We've been worried sick about you! Why did you run off like that? And where's that stupid dog?"

The 'stupid dog' appears at my words, trotting delightedly beside a boy about Kit's age, with a scruffy top that might once have been scarlet, but has obviously been bleached by the sun.

"Who--" I begin, taking a nervous step back.

Kit, whose face is the colour of the boy's shirt, nods breathlessly. "It's okay!" he says, patting Jack's arm. "He's not a pirate. This is Taishi."

"Tie..." Willow starts uncertainly, staring at the stranger with narrow, untrusting eyes.

"--Ishi," the stranger finishes for her. He is out of breath as well, but a lot less red than Kit. "I'd shake your hand, but we'd better find Two-legs. He <u>is</u> a pirate, but not the kind we need to be worrying about. "

He and Kit grin at each other. They are the same height, both with bony knees sticking out of dark grey shorts, and bony elbows sticking out of their too-small t-shirts. Somehow Kit looks as grubby as his new friend, even though Taishi has obviously been living outside. I can tell because he looks like he regularly goes swimming in the sea with his clothes on, and his hair is long and black and messy, as though it hasn't been cut for a long time. He looks Japanese but sounds American, and I wonder for the hundredth time what island we're on.

Taishi and Kit look at each other, both panting, and then Kit grabs Jack and Willow's elbows and starts to pull them back towards the window.

"Hang on," Jack says, yanking his arm free. "Aren't you going to explain where you've been?"

"Yes, but come on!" Kit is already halfway up the path, still dragging Willow behind him. "I'll tell you everything as soon as we're safe, but right now we have to run!"

Taishi speeds past me, nodding grimly. "Believe me, we don't want to get caught by these people."

We all start running back to the clearing then, with me trailing behind at the back. (*Again*.) Rounding the corner at a rush, I bump straight into Jack and Willow, who have stopped in their tracks at the sight of the most piratey-looking man I have ever seen. He's dark skinned and scowling, with long matted hair that swings past his shoulders. Golden hoops glint in both of his ears and his loose, dirty shirt is ripped in places. He's holding a hat in one hand, and where the other hand should've been is a shining hook.

"Oh!" I say, stupidly.

"Kit!" Jack hisses in panic, but Kit and Taishi are both grinning at the newcomer, bent over and trying to catch their breath. Beyond them is the window, a cool, breezy beacon of hope with the savoury scent still percolating through the air. Taishi edges towards it, though whether that's in desperation to escape or to get to the chicken, I can't tell.

"This is all of us," Kit pants, waving at me, Willow and Jack. "This is Johnny Two-Legs. He's the pirate," he adds, unnecessarily, indicating the man.

"Obviously," I mutter under my breath. Kit might *think* the danger is behind us, but I can't be sure yet that it isn't staring us in the face.

"It's a pleasure to meet you," Two-Legs says. He's soft spoken with a gentle West Country accent. Bristol, I think, although admittedly my knowledge of regional accents is patchy at best.

None of us say anything, so Kit hastily fills the silence by making introductions. "Johnny Two-Legs, Taishi, this is my brother Jack, who I was telling you about. And that's my cousin Willow, and Piper is my other cousin--she's the tall one with the plaits." We all wave weakly as Kit says our names in turn.

"Glad to make your acquaintance," John Two-Legs says. "Not sure about Two-Legs though, Kit. It's more like One-And-A-Half-Legs, just now."

Taishi twitches beside him. "Johnny!" he says, pointedly, eyeing the window.

Johnny Two-Legs--or One-And-A-Half-Legs, or whatever he's called--pats him reassuringly on the shoulder. "We've a few minutes, Taishi, lad. Those rascals have been caught in that rip tide and carried off round the headland. Be a while before they're back. They *will* be back, mind," he adds sternly, as though we suggested otherwise. "But we've time to catch our breaths, at least. Now, where was I?"

"Um..." Willow says. "Your name? The, er, one and a half legs?"

Johnny Two-Legs beams. "Of course. Now it's down but half a leg. Because of the cannon, see?"

I don't see at all, but it doesn't seem polite to say so. Anyway, I've had enough of not knowing what's going on, so to try and get things clear, I say, "Were you chasing us?"

"Well, to be truthful, it was young Taishi here doing the chasing," Johnny Two-Legs says.

"Yep, that was me." Taishi grins. "You'd be running too, if you'd been stuck on this island for months and months and your one chance to escape arrived at the *exact same moment* that Bembridge's ship appeared." He wipes a hand across his sweating brow and pats Silver, who is nudging his leg. "Soon as I saw Kit, I knew there had to be a way off this island. So, I ran after him."

"And I was only chasing Silver!" Kit says happily.

I frown at Taishi. "Right," I say slowly, trying to get things straight. "So, who exactly are you? Is this your island?"

"Feels like it," Johnny says, grinning at Taishi. "We've been here that long."

Taishi grins back. "Ever since we escaped from Bembridge, and that's... what do you think, Johnny? Longer than a year ago."

"Seventeen months, sonny," Johnny says. "Time flies."

"We're sailors," Taishi says. "I mean, Johnny is obviously a pirate..."

"I was a sailor first, boy," Johnny corrects.

"Well, yes, alright," Taishi says. "Johnny is a sailor, and I learned how to be a sailor, too, even though I didn't want to. And then we escaped from the ship we were on - it was a pirate ship - and we swam to this island with an empty barrel to keep us afloat."

"And we've been here ever since, lying low, hoping Bembridge doesn't come back alongside these shores," Johnny says, holding out his one hand to show that's the end of the story.

"Right," I say, glancing round at my sister and cousins to be sure they're following this, too. "So, *who* exactly is Bembridge and why should we be running away from them?"

Taishi and Johnny Two-Legs look meaningfully at each other, and a cloud passes over the sun, making us all shiver.

"Babs Bembridge," Taishi says softly, hunching his shoulders and glancing around nervously, "is the worst, most terrifying pirate to ever sail the ocean."

I feel Kit lean in a little closer to me. His eyes are huge and round, and the smile has gone from his face. "Taishi told me she takes children," he whispers.

I resist the urge to look behind me, but my shoulder blades have an icy feeling, as though someone holding a knife to them. I take a deep, fortifying breath of the cool air that is streaming from the window behind me. "Don't be silly," I say firmly, trying to inject some normality into our tight, nervous little group.

Jack nudges me sharply. "We're on a desert island *inside a house*," he says, pointing at the window. "I think at this point just about anything's possible."

I shiver once more and glance at my sister. Willow has goosebumps all up her arms and is looking anxiously from me to the pirate and back again.

"What does she take them for?" she asks, her voice a tiny breath on the cooling breeze from the window.

Taishi answers. "To work in her gold mines," he says. "And to feed her creature." He wraps his arms around himself, his scarlet sleeves flapping in the wind. Obviously, the weather at Merryshields isn't as bright and sunny as it is here, on the island. I look at the sky through the window. It's grey and the clouds are thick, sweeping quickly across the sky.

"Bembridge is known as the Witch of The Seas," Johnny Two-Legs says. "She's known as such across all the oceans of the world, and if I'd known it was her ship, I would never have taken my feet off the Bristol dock. But when I boarded her vessel not quite two years ago, I thought it was a merchant ship run by a local ship-owner, sailing for coffee and cocoa from the islands."

"Are you from Bristol, too?" Jack asks Taishi. He shakes his head, but looks at Johnny, letting the old sailor continue. Johnny Two-Legs is looking at us, but his eyes look like they're looking back in the past.

"We were far into the Atlantic before the truth became clear. Babs had stayed below-deck, out of sight of the witch-catchers on shore who would have pulled her up before the courts, had they got her. And when I found out... well, I felt tricked. I couldn't believe I had fallen for it..."

"It wasn't your fault," Taishi says, sounding quite grown up for a kid. "You couldn't have known."

"Well, I intended to jump ship each port we came into, but was prevented at every turn. First the quarter-master had it in for me, then I had wicked food poisoning, kept me from leaving my berth, never mind the ship. And by the time I was fit and able again, well - they'd pulled into Taishi's islands and he'd been hauled aboard..."

"Me and twenty others," Taishi interrupts, and Willow goes even paler.

"I couldn't save them all," Johnny says. "The monster had some of them, 'fore we got close to land. But Taishi here, he snuck away with me as soon as we were within sight of this isle."

"We thought better to risk our chances here in the unknown, than spend another minute on that ship with that witch," Taishi says. "And then a few days ago, that window popped up!"

"Only a few days ago?" Kit asks, just as I say,

"The *monster*?"

Taishi nods at Kit. "I was all for jumping straight through it, but Johnny said it might be an alien world that we would never make it back from." He peers up at the weatherbeaten man beside him, looking half-exasperated and half-affectionate.

I think answering the monster question is more important than the window one, but they've moved on before I can open my mouth again.

"Couldn't let him just leap into more danger," Johnny Two-Legs says, a little gruffly. "Best to sit tight and wait a few days, and watch; see if there was any danger before we left the island for pastures new. Even if the smell of that roast chicken did almost make me climb out myself, one arm or no."

I breathed in automatically. The smell of roast chicken was still there - Silver was sitting with his nose pointing straight at the window - but there was a lot of rain in the air, too. A gust of wind sent it showering across my bare arms, making me shiver in the warm air.

"About this monster," I begin, but Taishi has started talking.

"But now the Witch of the Seas is *back*," he says, his feet shuffling against the sand as though desperate to carry him away. "You see, she's not just called a witch because of how cruel she is--she really *is* a witch. She's got this crazy power: she holds out her fingers..."

"Like this," Johnny Two-Legs offers, demonstrating with his one hand by wiggling his fingers out in front of him.

"And then she sort of...*senses* where the things that she wants are."

"Treasure. Gold," Johnny Two-Legs says, his tone grave. "Makes the hair stand up on the back of my neck to see her do it, and that's the truth."

"And she steals children," Taishi says.

"Steals the kiddies that get caught in her path," Johnny Two-Legs says. "Takes them from their homes and uses them for her mining and never sits 'em free."

"And she's *here*, Johnny," Taishi repeats insistently.

The wind from the other side of the window is really picking up, now, making the leaves of the trees around us rustle alarmingly. It occurs to me that if someone were to sneak up on us now, we'd never hear them in all this noise.

"What do we do?" I ask, trying not to sound frantic in front of Kit and Willow.

"Johnny Two-Legs didn't see the door on the beach," Kit says. "But now we've got the window! So we can all get to safety - and then shut the window behind us. Bembridge won't be able to get any of us."

"How does the window help us get to safety?" I snap. "It's four stories up!"

Kit and Taishi look at each other.

"Well," Kit says slowly, his eyes flicking towards Jack. "I thought that maybe - just maybe - I could climb out of it..."

"What?!" Jack explodes. "Are you mad?"

Willow grabs Jack's arm. Her face is pale, but she's nodding. "He's right," she says. "It's the only way. One of us has to climb out, get along to the next window, climb back in..."

"And open the door again," I finish, my voice hollow. I knew it would have to be me.

Johnny Two-Legs

Kit

J ack is FURIOUS with me for running off after Silver, but I don't think I could have *not* run after him. It's like I was attached to him on invisible elastic--so when he ran, I had to run, too. At first, I thought Silver was barking at the pirate snoozing in his hammock, but he sprinted straight past him and up the beach. The people in the rowing boat were all black hats and glinting daggers, waving their arms and pointing. I was sure they were here for the treasure - I mean, this must be where Merryshields is keeping that big treasure chest, so it makes sense that other people are trying to find it, too. The sailors looked like they were struggling to get across the reef, but with three of them I thought it wouldn't take long. It was hard running on the sand. I thought my legs had stopped working for a while; it was like when you're running in a dream and it's really slow. But then I glanced behind me to see if Jack and the others were following me, and I saw the pirate! The sun was behind him, so I couldn't see his face, just the big black shape of his hat and his hook that he was waving up in the air as though he were going to pick me up with it. Then, there was a boy who raced out of the trees and joined the chase. His face was fierce and he was sprinting as fast as he could.

Suddenly I found I could run much faster.

Silver was still galloping ahead and I didn't have the breath to shout for him, so I just kept going, following him. I was so relieved when he led me into the shade. He had paused to wait for me at the start of a well-trodden track. I glanced behind me as I puffed onwards. The pirate had vanished, but the boy was still there, though I thought he was a bit further away. I was obviously a better runner than him. I caught up to Silver and we raced along the path together, the silly dog's ears flapping and his tail wagging like mad, as though it was all a big game. I was just worrying about how on earth I was going to find everyone again, because I had no idea of how far we'd gone. But then I smelled chicken, and we found the window (I'm pretty sure Silver was running *because* he could smell the roast chicken) and I was so surprised and out of breath that I didn't know what to do next. So I scrambled into some bushes like the ones we had slept in overnight, and watched.

The boy came a few minutes after me. He stopped in the clearing to catch his breath and looked all around. He was about my age, but a lot messier. His hair was long and his shirt was untucked and he was definitely what my mam calls grubby (usually when I've had a really nice day outside and she spoils it by saying I ought to have a bath). Anyway, he put his fingers in his mouth and gave a massive whistle, and I made a mental note to learn how to do that. At his whistle, the three red birds we'd seen earlier came fluttering through the leaves and landed on a branch close by, all watching him. Then he shouted, "JOHNNY! TWO-LEGS, WHERE ARE YOU?"

Before I could wonder why on earth someone would shout for a person's leg - never mind both of them - my heart jumped out of my throat as a heavy hand landed on my shoulder and a deep voice rumbled behind me.

"Right here, lad. And I've got the little one and his dog, here, too."

I looked round in horror, trying to wriggle free, but he had me gripped tightly. It was the pirate we had spent all night avoiding. How we didn't see the boy around the campsite, I don't know. Silver, the traitor, was nosing at the pirate's knees, so the man loosened his grip on me to bend down and scratch his ears.

That's how I knew he couldn't be too bad.

"Thank you for stopping, young man," he said, though I hadn't really had a choice. "Not sure I could've carried on chasing round the jungle after you. Got a bad knee from a cannon shot."

My mouth dropped open. I couldn't help it; it was just such an unexpected thing to say.

"Did you get hit?" I asked. I thought you'd have <u>no</u> knee if it got hit by a cannonball, but I might have been wrong.

"Went straight past me ear," he said. "Fell off the rigging and landed on me knee." He slapped his leg. "Never been the same since."

"Oh," I said. I definitely wanted to hear more, but was interrupted by the boy shoving his way through the undergrowth. He was smiling widely.

"Was just whistling for the birds," he said to the pirate. To me he said admiringly, "You're fast."

I shrugged. "I know." I smiled as I said it, so it didn't sound too boastful. "My name's Kit," I said, "and that's my dog Silver. What's yours?"

"Taishi," the boy said.

"Taishi," I repeated carefully, wanting to get it right. Then I looked at the pirate.

"Johnny Two-Legs," he said. "On account of having two legs, see?"

I looked at his hook, and he shrugged. "Johnny One-Arm was taken," he said. "I'm sorry if I scared you, Kit lad, but you're the first person we've seen in seventeen months. Now those scallywags have turned up in the bay, we really need to set our noses to the wind and make shift to get off this island, fast as we can."

"Seventeen months?" I asked, astonished. "Have you really been here all that time?"

Johnny Two-Legs and Taishi nodded grimly. "We abandoned ship amidst a storm, winter before last," Johnny Two-Legs said.

"We had to escape the witch and her crew," Taishi added. "It was worth it, being stuck here instead of with her, but there's only so much fish and coconuts you can eat, and now-"

"Witch?" I interrupted, sure that I was hearing things. Then Silver pricked his ears and woofed at something I couldn't hear. "Wait - tell me in a minute - I have to get the others!"

"Others?" Johnny Two-Legs asked.

"How did you get here?" Taishi said at the same time.

"Through the door," I said, searching for the path to get me back to camp. "But it vanished straightaway when Willow closed it."

"What door?" said Johnny Two-Legs.

"What others?" said Taishi.

I shoved my way back to the window, the two strangers following. "Let's get back to camp and we'll tell you everything," I said, peering out of the window as we passed. "Wow, this is so weird! I *have* to show Jack."

Taishi grabbed my elbow. "If the others are at *our* campsite..." he said, his words trailing off so it sounded like a question. I nodded at him to continue so he went on, "... then Two-Legs should go back this way, it's quicker." He pointed to a path that led into the jungle. "It's goes through the trees to get back to the campsite," he explained.

"And if they've chased you down the beach, you and Taishi should go that way, and cut them off," Johnny Two-Legs said, pointing to a narrow track between two coconuts. "That'll take you back towards the beach, directly. You two go on ahead. I'll stomp back to camp." He started walking and then turned. "Whistle if you find them, and I'll do the same," he said to Taishi, and Taishi nodded. Then the pirate disappeared among the trees.

I felt a little flutter of urgency, thinking of Jack looking for me, so when Taishi said, "Ready to run again?" I said yes immediately. So we ran, and he told me all about Babs Bembridge and I told him all about the door and the others, and by the time we caught up with everybody, I was both exhausted and terrified. At least we were all together again, even though it looks like we are in MORTAL PERIL.

And even though Jack is still ABSOLUTELY MAD with me.

Now, of course, we are waiting and watching as Piper tries to find her balance on the sill of the window. Taishi and I keep glancing around, hoping that the other pirates don't creep up behind us.

"I wish it could be me," Johnny Two-Legs says apologetically. "If I'd known it was safe - and if it weren't for me gammy knee and me hook - I'd have done it meself days ago as soon as this window popped up."

"I would have done it anytime," Taishi said, a bit crossly. "Only Johnny wouldn't let me."

"Not rescuing you off that ship just to see you smashed to blood and guts all over that gravel," the pirate said gruffly. "Oh - sorry, maid..."

"It's alright," Piper says, although she doesn't really look alright. "Just... just don't look, okay? I mean..." she swallows. "If I fall, there's nothing you can do anyway, so you may as well not watch."

Willow is crying. I have a huge lump in my throat. Even Jack has gone pale and shiny.

"Come on, now," Johnny Two-Legs says, taking out a grubby hanky and handing it to Willow. "Dry your eyes. We'll all stand here as still as anything and think holding-on thoughts. Your sister'll be right as rain."

I hope he's right.

Big Trouble

Willow

It is absolutely the most awful feeling ever, watching Piper climb out of that window. She sits on the ledge for a few seconds and I can see that she's gearing herself up to carry on. The thing is, Piper's never been much good with heights. She doesn't really like it when we go over bridges, and she would definitely <u>never</u> go on a Ferris wheel. But she takes her role as the eldest of the four of us very seriously - even though Jack isn't that much younger, Piper would never let him do something so dangerous. She thinks it's her job to look after us and keep us safe, and although that's sometimes annoying, secretly I think it's sometimes really lovely of her, too. She's actually a lot braver than people think.

She looks back at me, and I know that she's really, really scared, but she clenches her jaw and nods, and I nod back. And then she turns around.

As soon as she stands up, I take a step closer.

"But Piper said..." Kit starts.

"Shut up," Jack hisses.

Taishi doesn't say anything at all. Nor does Johnny Two-Legs. He's standing by the window with a stern expression on the bit of his face that I can see under all the hair, and his hand's stretched a little bit out, as though he's waiting, ready to grab hold of Piper and stop her from falling if he needs to. I watch Piper's feet move across the sill and jump as a bird flies past her. I gulp, but I don't make a sound. It seems even *higher*, now that she's actually out there.

We listen in silence, hardly daring to breathe as we strain our ears to hear to the small sound of her feet shuffling along. It's raining now and the wind is whistling, making it really hard to hear what's going on. The windowsill is a narrow shelf of stone stretching all the way around the top of the house. The only thing Piper has to hold on to is the rickety old guttering that runs along under the roof. I try not to think of Mum, who looked up at it the day we moved in and threw her arms up in despair. "That whole lot's going to have to come down, Seren; it'll not last one single rainstorm!" is what she had said. I hope she was wrong.

I take a deep breath and cross all my fingers, then tiptoe across the sand until I can reach out and put my hand on the window frame. I don't want to distract Piper, but I don't care what she said; I can't *not* watch. Beside me is a flutter of red feathers, and then one of the parrots lands on my shoulder and gently pecks my ear.

"Never thought I'd see the day when me old flag would get me <u>out</u> of trouble instead of into it," Johnny Two-Legs broaches into the silence. He sounds jolly, and I know he's trying to keep all of us calm by making conversation.

Kit's voice sounds only a tiny bit wobbly. "Have you been waving it a lot?"

"Every day since we first found the window," Taishi replies. "Between four bells and two bells. We have to imagine when the second bell is, but I've got pretty good at reading the sun by now."

"That's right. Noon and the second - or whenever me arm falls asleep!" Two-Legs chuckles. "Sometimes I leave me hook off and wedge that out the window, so's we can leave it a bit longer. But we never saw another human out there."

"You didn't see us yesterday, then? In the trees, down there?" Jack points toward the orchard.

"Nope," says Taishi. I hear the rustle of Two-Legs's hat as he shakes his head.

I look over my shoulder at the group. Jack is ripping a palm leaf into shreds, scattering them carelessly onto the sand. He's afraid for Piper, too. He always fiddles with things, rips up paper and stuff, when he's worrying. Kit has reached out for my hand and we are squeezing tightly, as though each of us is holding Piper to keep her up.

My attention is ripped back to my sister as I hear her shriek. Piper's foot lurches and she grips tightly onto the slippery drainpipe, which creaks ominously. I clutch the windowsill and lean out, willing with all my might for her to get to the next window safely. I don't dare say a word to her, or look down, either. It's such a long way up. But she is getting closer...

"Last few days, we started smelling food on the wind coming in this window," Taishi says.

She's almost there...

"But then Bembridge's ship showed up on the horizon..." says Johnny Two-Legs.

One of her hands holds the top of the next-door window...she has one foot almost completely on the sill...

"And we knew we were in trouble if Bembridge landed here," Taishi continued.

Piper moves to unlatch the window, when two arms appear from inside and haul her out of sight.

"Piper!" I shout.

A voice, familiar in its terrifying fury, rumbles towards us at a hundred decibels.

"JUST WHAT ON EARTH DO YOU THINK YOU'RE DO-ING, YOUNG LADY? WHERE IS YOUR SISTER? AND YOUR COUSINS?"

My heart rises and sinks at the same time. I turn to the others. The boys' eyes are wide with excitement at Piper's success and fear of my mum.

I can't hear Piper's reply. I imagine she's so relieved at having made it that she can't actually speak. How unlucky is she, to have got to the window at the precise moment our mum is in that very room? Out of all the *hundreds* of rooms in the house! Mum's voice comes again, at supersonic sound.

"WHAT DO YOU MEAN, THEY'RE NEXT DOOR?! I'VE JUST <u>BEEN</u> NEXT DOOR! THAT ROOM IS EMPTY!"

Finally, Piper's voice, shaky but clear--and clearly directed at me. I gesture furiously at the boys.

"They must still be hiding!" Piper tries desperately to explain. "We were playing hide and seek and I thought I'd hide somewhere they'd never find me, but I expect they're on their way back to the door *right now*!" She says the last two words deliberately and slowly.

"WHAT ON EARTH DO YOU MEAN, BACK TO THE DOOR?"

I leap to my feet. "Come on!"

Luckily, everyone understands. Kit starts to run backwards through the jungly undergrowth, grabbing Taishi's elbow.

"What about Johnny Two-Legs and Taishi?" he asks.

"We'll come back for you!" I am running backwards too, calling as I go. Taishi is jogging alongside Kit, an anxious frown on his face.

"I promise, alright?" I say, looking deep into his eyes. "Johnny Two-Legs, Taishi, we *promise* we'll come back as soon as we can! As soon as it's dark! We'll shout from the door - oh, you've never seen it - Taishi, you'll see it in a minute! It's near your campsite, on the beach! But if we don't go now, we'll be in more trouble than we've ever been in before and we might not be able to ever get back to you!"

We're already out of sight of the window clearing. I can just see Johnny Two-Legs, still standing beside the eerie frame, his hat in his hand, staring after us hopefully.

"Soon as you can, mateys? Promise!" he calls.

Jack yells as he dives headfirst through the bushes. "We promise! Once it's dark! Don't get caught and wait for us!"

"I'll follow them and see where to go, Two-Legs!" Taishi calls.

We run as fast as we can, hurtling through the leaves and onto the beach in a matter of seconds. We have no time to marvel at how close the window had been all along. The *second* we step onto the sand, the door appears in the air in front of us. As we reach it, panting madly, the sounds of doom and fury make our immediate future horribly clear.

Even The House Is Cross

Jack

W e are in the worst trouble we have ever been in, in the whole of our lives.

You would not *believe* the amount of shouting and yelling. Mam and Dad shouting at me and Kit. Auntie Percy shouting at the girls. All three of them shouting at all four of us at the same time. And the worst of it is, we can't give them any answers (at least none they will believe). The only thing we can *truthfully* say is that we've been in the house the whole time. Which doesn't help.

There's an awful lot of WHAT DID YOU THINK YOU WERE PLAYING AT, STAYING OUT ALL NIGHT?! and HOW DID YOU NOT HEAR US SHOUTING FOR YOU?! and WHICH FIREPLACE DID YOU BUILD A FIRE IN?! (That last one confuses us for ages, until we realise we smell of woodsmoke, having been so close to Two-Legs' campfire all night.) The moment they stop shouting long enough for us to reply, we mutter guiltily that we were playing an elaborate game of hide and seek--like Piper said - and it got a bit out of hand, and that we'd opened a window and someone must have been burning leaves somewhere. I don't think for a second that they believe this last bit - they lectured us for ages when we first moved in about the dangers of playing with fire, because there are fireplaces in *all* the rooms and I guess they thought we'd just get too tempted to use one - but thank goodness Dad says that he smelled burning leaves, too, because the farmer over the hill had been having a bonfire. He then says he found this out BECAUSE I HAD TO GO

LOOKING FOR YOU IN THE WOODS! And we all feel really guilty all over again.

"As if we haven't got enough to worry about," Mam says tearfully. Her eyes are red and her hair is all over the place, and she's put her cardigan on inside out, which is so unlike her that it makes my tummy feel really twisty. "Your Great Auntie Glynis has taken a turn for the worse and Uncle Toby can't come back until autumn at the earliest, and I might have to go back to work..." She sniffs.

Auntie Percy says, "And that's before we even begin to talk about what you did in the kitchen."

We don't dare to look at each other, but I know we're all thinking the same thing. What on earth has happened in the kitchen?

We don't have to wait long to find out.

We're hauled downstairs, being shouted at all the way, and shown the kitchen, where it appears that there has been an explosion and a tsunami and a food hurricane all at once. There is food EVERYWHERE. And containers, and plates, and packets, and cutlery... water and milk and teabags and cornflakes... tea towels, washing up liquid, shopping lists and all kinds of utensils that I've never seen before and can't even imagine what they might be used for. All of it is all over the place.

"Chicken," Kit breathes, as we spy a huge roast chicken on the counter, still steaming, as though it is fresh out of the oven. My tummy hurts with hunger. Silver's tail is wagging so hard it's banging against my legs, but thankfully, he doesn't jump up and start scoffing it. The Olds can't see him, but I'm pretty sure they'd notice if a chicken started disappearing before their eyes.

They are still in full flow, though. They make us come all the way into the kitchen, where we have to stand in a line and LOOK AT ALL THE MESS YOU HAVE CAUSED. HAVE YOU ANY IDEA HOW LONG IT'S GOING TO TAKE TO CLEAR THIS LOT UP?

"Oh, you will," Dad says grimly. His glasses are wonky and he keeps putting his hand on Mam's shoulder, though I don't know if it's to comfort her or to stop her getting so angry that she explodes. "You will," he repeats, "because you're going to do it. For the rest of the day. Until it's *done*. And if you can find enough food to make sandwiches, you'll be lucky."

We stand in our line looking at them standing in a line looking at us. Auntie Percy has obviously been running her hands through her hair all night because it's really bushy and wild. She looks like she doesn't know whether to cry or to yell. It's understandable, I suppose. Mam and Dad can be angry and afraid together, like a team, but Auntie Percy has to feel everything all on her own. It must be pretty tiring. The girls are standing next to me and they've both got tears running down their faces. I can feel Piper shaking. I'm guessing it's not just the telling off. She was amazing, climbing between the windows like that.

When the Olds finally leave the kitchen, we all slump down at the table. Piper leans into Willow, who hugs her tightly. The kitchen rings with silence now that the shouting's stopped, but I can still hear it all echoing through my head. Mam and dad must have been frantic all night worrying about us. My heart sinks right through my tummy.

"What are we going to do?" I ask into the silence.

The others look like I feel. Nobody says anything for a moment, and then Willow looks over Piper's head, around the kitchen and back at us again.

"Well," she says. "We need to help Two-Legs, and if we're going to make it up to the Olds, we really need to find that treasure. Please, house?" she adds, slightly sheepishly. "But before we can do any of that, we're going to have to tackle this kitchen."

I swear if the house could turn its back on us, it just did.

Everyone takes a deep breath. I survey the damage with my captain's eyes. I can see why the Olds are so mad.

Every single cupboard in the enormous kitchen is open and I can smell a hundred smells in the air. The cupboards are half-empty, contents spilling out all over the surfaces and onto the floor: open packets, sauce bottles dripping on their sides, a cloud of flour hanging over the sink. A trail of ants is busy transferring sugar from one of side of the kitchen to the other. Cardboard boxes filled with the kitchen items from when we moved in are on their sides, contents strewn all over the place. Along the top of the radiator, Dad's mackerel lie in a line, making the whole room smell fishy. Instead of saucepans hanging from the hooks on the wall, there are slices of ham. All the mixing bowls are stacked dangerously on a patch of oil on the tiles.

I am known for being a little messy, but even I have never seen anything like it.

"What on earth happened in here?" Piper breathes.

"I think the house is cross with us, just like our parents," Kit says.

"I think you're right," I say. There is a definite feeling of cross disappointment in the air, and it's not just the leftover anger from the Olds. I sigh and look at my fingers, sticky from where I put my hand in some jam smeared down the back of the chair. None of us can deny that the house is beginning to act a bit like an actual person. A person who usually likes us and gives us amazing things... and a person who we've now really, really annoyed.

"Well, it's no use sitting and staring at it," Willow says, pushing her chair back. "Come on. We'd better get started."

It really does take us the whole day. Even once we've:

•Tidied up the cornflakes / rice pops / crispy puffs
•Turned all the dripping bottles upright
•Swept up all the dried pasta and rice
•Stopped Silver walking through the honey-ketchup-pickle mixture

•Retrieved the smelly fish from the radiator. (And the larder steps. *And* the big upside-down poles where our wellies would be if they weren't at the bottom of a river.)

•Rescued as much food as we can from the open packets spilling all over the floor

•Disentangled all the kitchen utensils which are hanging around the walls like tinsel

•Found out why the larder smells of garlic powder and pickled cabbage

•Washed up, dried up and wiped all the surfaces

Yes, even after *all of that,* the Olds laugh darkly and say that since all the cupboards are more or less empty, we may as well clean them out. And scrub the hob. And all the shelves and racks and surfaces and everything else in the entire room. I don't know if anyone else has told you about the kitchen, but let me just say, it's massive. It's not surprising given how enormous the house is, but you really realise it when you've got to clean every single centimetre.

We have to endure the smell of the Old's Chinese takeaway, which they collect when they take the beautiful chicken over to Great-Auntie Glynis's house, while we make our own tea with the only things we can find: half a loaf of bread and some old mushroom paste. That shows how hungry we are. Piper even goes to ask the Olds about sandwiches, but she returns shaking her head gloomily. We look for ages for some butter, until Kit finds it balancing on a drawer handle in the pantry, half melted and dripping all over the floor, covered in ants.

"Actually, Silver found it," Kit says cheerfully. We had tried to stop Silver from going all over the place and getting his paws into everything, but as Willow pointed out, he was slurping everything up which was actually quite helpful.

We eat at the table. We're exhausted and grimy round the edges and, even though it's not Chinese takeaway, the mushroom paste sandwich is actually really yummy. (Though that's probably more a measure of how ravenous we are since we haven't eaten all day or all night *or* most of yesterday.) Nobody says very much. There's still an air of enormous disapproval, and it's coming from the house itself. Willow looks like she wants to say something about it, but when she opens her mouth and puts her hand flat on the table, a dish slips in the soapy water still left in the sink at the other end of the room. It makes us all jump, and Willow closes her mouth again and lifts her hand up with a little grimace.

We find one solitary packet of chocolate fingers at the very back of the pantry, but even though our mouths are watering, Piper puts them sadly onto a high shelf and closes the door.

"We'd really better not," she says.

I agree with her. "They're the last packet from Dad's birthday, before we moved," I tell her. "The Olds'll probably want to have them when... you know... everyone's a bit happier."

At the end of the day, kitchen sparkling in the setting sun and crewmates drained and weary, we are finally forgiven by Mam and Dad and Auntie Percy, and are allowed to roam free after making a thousand promises to never disappear again. When the Olds leave the kitchen, hot steamy mugs of Horlicks in their hands, Piper scowls tiredly at the room.

"If you could help us the slightest bit, house, it would be easier to keep our promises!" she says. "It wasn't *completely* our fault we got stuck on that island!"

The air above the table shimmers and then, very gently, there appears a bunch of grapes, a plum, an apricot and a banana.

Immediately, the air feels brighter and happier.

"Alright then," I say, and gently tap the table in thanks. "Thank you." And taking the fruit with us, we drag ourselves up to bed.

Return To The Island

Piper

I could have slept for a whole week after all of that clean-ing. Not to mention the wild night awake beneath the whispering palms of an almost-deserted island. But, since I always hate getting up anyway, and the boys are impossible to shift in the mornings, Willow volunteered to set her alarm for midnight and wake us up. She wakes up all the way as soon as she opens her eyes. I don't know how she does it. It takes me ages to get going. I have to admit, though, that I am glad to have been woken up this time. I'd been dreaming of that awful climb from window to window--only in the dream I kept slipping, over and over, falling and tumbling down before jerking almost-awake, only to repeat it all over again.

As soon as Willow shakes me gently by the shoulder, I prop myself up, relieved that I am back in the real world. Outside, the wind is 'blowing a hooly', as Dad would say, and the rain is spattering against the windows. I squeeze her hand in thanks, and she goes across to the boys' room to wake them, too, while I pull on my clothes.

"Come on," she whispers, when we finally gather on the silent landing. "I've got everything we need; we just have to hurry!"

"What've you got?" Kit asks, stumbling sleepily behind us as we scurry, quiet as mice, along the corridor towards the stairs that will take us to the island room. "What do we need?"

"Can I smell roast chicken again?" Jack asks, sniffing. "Where on earth did you get that?! Surely the Olds didn't cook another one after they ate all that Chinese food."

"I'm guessing it was Mrs B," Willow whispers. "It was on the kitchen table in a basket with a little label that said, 'Johnny.'"

"How does she know about Johnny Two-Legs?" I wonder out loud.

"I expect the house told her," Kit says importantly. "The house *knows*." He looks down at Silver trotting beside him. "Don't make any noise this time," he tells the dog warningly. "We can't have that Bembridge or any of her crew knowing we're on the island." Silver noses him gently on the leg in understanding.

"Don't worry," I say grimly. "You're staying on the *house* side of the door to make sure we don't get trapped again!"

Kit looks like he wants to complain, but he puts his lips together and nods, and I sigh a private breath of relief. I don't ever want to feel like I did when I thought he was gone - never again.

Willow pulls a torch out of her pocket as we open the door to the staircase. "You really have thought of everything!" I say, admiringly.

She grins at me over her shoulder. "I've been up for ages," she said. "Made sure the Olds were completely asleep before I did anything, then I packed my bag and got all the food ready."

The stairs seem to climb much higher than they had the day before, but maybe that's because we're going more slowly in the dark. My legs ache. It isn't much lighter at the top of the stairs, but at least it's flat.

Jack yawns. "That was the longest day in the history of days," he says.

"Isn't it still today?" Kit asks, yawning too. "Or is it tomorrow?"

"*Technically*, it's tomorrow," I tell him, "but it *feels* like it's still today."

"I can't believe that when we woke up this morning, we were on a desert island," Willow says, shining the torch at her own face. She looks really creepy, with dark hollows under her cheekbones and huge purple shadows for eyebags, but her eyes still shine with excitement and she has a huge smile on her face. "It feels so much better to think about it now that we're safe!"

"I hope Two-Legs and Taishi are safe, too," Kit says, worried. "Do you think the other pirates got them?"

Jack and I look at each other.

"Nah, I bet they managed to fight them off," Jack says robustly. "Two-Legs is a pirate, after all, and Taishi seemed pretty tough."

"But there were more than two of the enemy pirates," Willow reminds him. "And *they* haven't been living on an island for seventeen months, surviving on just coconuts and fish."

"Yeah! *And* Two-Legs has a hook instead of a hand. *And* a gammy knee," Kit adds. "And Taishi might be tough, but he's not *that* fast. Besides, even if he could run away, I don't think he would. He wouldn't leave Two-Legs behind."

We all start walking faster.

"Come on," Jack says after a minute. "We're far enough away now that the Olds won't hear us. Let's run."

We break into a sprint down the corridor, ending up panting outside the last door. I put my hand on the handle. It feels warm and smooth. With one determined glance at the others, I turn the knob as slowly and quietly as I can, and push it open.

The sea slides up and down the moonlit sand. The tide is coming in, and the waves almost reach the doorframe. The sky is as thick with stars as it was the night before, and looks even more beautiful now that we know we don't have to stay here.

"Right," I whisper. "Me and Jack will go over to the campsite. Willow, you wait here and hold the door open-" I glare at her to make sure she understands, and she nods sheepishly. "And Kit, you and Silver stay here and keep lookout. Right?"

Kit stands up straighter. "Ok."

"Keep hold of Silver!" I warn him.

Everyone looks at Silver, then back at me. Kit puts his fingers firmly through Silver's collar and the dog sits beside him like a good boy, even though his tail is quivering and he is clearly longing to gambol around the empty beach.

"Right," I say again, a little sharply, before anyone gets any ideas. "We don't want to be here any longer than we have to be. Jack, is that pirate ship still there?"

Jack peers around the edge of the door and nods. "Yep," he says. "I can't see the rowing boat, though."

"Well, we can't help that right now," I say. "Is everyone ready? Johnny Two-Legs and Taishi ought to be nearby, so this shouldn't take too long. Let's go." I grab Jack's arm and we step back onto the desert island we had been trying so hard to escape from just hours before.

It feels terrifying to move away from the safety of the door. We are exposed; the moonlight is bright and there are no clouds in the sky. The jungly undergrowth seems menacing somehow, as though it's hiding hundreds of pirates just out of sight, waiting to capture us and drag us off to Bembridge's waiting ship. It won't matter what the others do if we get captured - nothing would be able to save us.

I pick up my pace slightly and feel Jack adjust his steps in turn. He must have been feeling the same, for even though I let his arm go, he is walking so close to me his arm is brushing against mine, and his face is set like stone in the moonlight.

"Didn't seem so far away in the daylight, did it?" he mutters quietly.

"We should be able to see it from here," I whisper, peering into the darkness.

"I expect he put the fire out," Jack breathes. We are close enough now that we can smell damp vegetation, wet charred wood and a faint smoky, fishy scent. "Easier to hide from the pirates."

"If he *is* hiding." An awful thought strikes me and I grab Jack's arm again. "Jack, do you really think Two-Legs and Taishi were here alone for all that time? I mean, what if it was a trap and they're just waiting to catch us and take us to Bembridge themselves?!"

His step falters for a second as he thinks about this, but he shakes it off quickly.

"Nobody could have known we were going to come through that door--they didn't even know the door was there."

"So they *say*."

"No, Piper - if they'd known, they wouldn't have waited, would they? They would have just have walked through. They couldn't have known we were coming. No, I think Two-Legs and Taishi are telling the truth. But I wish I knew where they were. Knowing that ship is on the horizon is giving me the creeps."

"We're right here." A voice, deep and scratchy, comes out of the undergrowth, and I let out a breathy scream. Jack elbows me sharply in the ribs.

"Get a grip," he says. "It's only Two-Legs."

The pirate looms out of the darkness, a shadow against the night. A bag has been flung over one shoulder and something small moves at his side. Three shadows swoop through the air behind him, wings fluttering soundlessly.

"Best move quickly, mateys," Taishi murmurs. "Those rapscallions are roaming around the island looking for a likely place to come ashore."

"Have they not landed?" Jack asks in surprise.

"Oho, yes," Johnny Two-Legs says, "but they need fresh water for the ship and there's only one place to find it. They'll need to sail around the other side of the island, where there's a break in the reef. They only sent the rowboat to the bay because they saw our fire, ya see? I overheard the scurvy dogs talking as I was hidden in the bushes backalong. They think they've time to flush us out and take us along with 'em. But there's only ever one of the three on watch; let's not give them time to raise the alarm."

We rush back across the sand. Willow is fidgeting at the door, agitated; as we get closer, she hisses, "Hurry! I saw a light, through the trees!"

Taishi runs ahead to clasp Kit by the hand as he crosses the threshold. Johnny Two-Legs limps after him as fast as he can, Jack and I willing him on over the fine sand. I look around as we fall back through the door. Willow is right. In the middle of the jungle, a fiery torch burns and a shout rings out, "The shore! To the shore!"

Willow pulls the door closed after us with a decisive click, and the sound of the sea is deadened at once. I can still smell salt on the air and my heart is hammering in my chest, reminding me of how real it all is. I push against the door with the heel of my hand, just to check. It stays reassuringly closed.

"Well, thank goodness for that!" I say.

Silly Dog

Kit

None of us want to stay near the island room, even though the door is definitely shut.

"I wish it had a lock!" I say, but Jack and Piper are too out of breath to hear me, and Willow is busy saying something to Johnny Two-Legs about chicken. I follow them along the corridor, walking alongside Taishi who doesn't seem to feel like speaking, and into a little room that none of us has been in before.

Then I realise a very important and very *worrying* thing.

"SILVER!" I gasp.

Piper whirls around.

"Where is he?" she asks.

I spin on the spot, but I know he isn't here. He's never been very far away from me... apart from that one time on the beach.

"I don't know!" I say. I can feel my face getting wobbly and clench my teeth together.

Jack puts his hand on my shoulder. "He must have snuck onto the beach through the door when we came back through," he says. "Come on, hopefully he'll be just on the other side."

My heart feels like it has dropped all the way through my chest and tummy and all the way down to my feet. I know the others are angry about having to open the door again. I don't want to, either. But the thought of Silver being stuck there on his own, maybe being stolen by the pirates and taken away to be a ship's dog, makes the tears well in my eyes. Jack pulls me into a rare hug.

"We'll find him," he whispers, so only I can hear. "He won't have gone far. He's probably running around the beach looking for you."

I hope he's right.

We go back to the door and Willow smiles at me as she put her ear against it.

"I can't hear anything," she says. "I mean, I can hear the sea, but I can't hear any voices." She and Piper look at each other, and then Piper opens the door. There is the beach and the sea and the trees - and even though I know that's what I'm going to see, it still makes my mouth fall open in shock a bit. It's just so strange.

Piper steps quickly onto the sand to peek behind the door. "Silver!" she calls. "Come on, boy!"

Johnny Two-Legs pushes me forward. "Go on, son," he says. "He's your dog, he'll be listening for you."

So I follow Piper just over the threshold, Jack holding tightly to my pyjamas, and shout as loud as I dare, "SILVER! COME ON, YOU SILLY DOG!"

We wait, listening to the tropical breeze on the island and the cold, rainy wind outside Merryshields. Voices shout from the jungle, and the torch lights Willow saw earlier start jogging as the person holding it begins to run through the trees. Then I hear a bark from the middle of the island.

"The window!" Taishi says suddenly, springing forward and gripping Willow's shoulder. "Where's that window?"

"Oh!" she says, and drags him into the room next door. I was torn between wanting to follow them and wanting to stay on the beach in case Silver comes this way.

"What's going on with Willow and Taishi?" I ask Jack. He listens hard, still not letting go of my pyjamas. I know he's ready to pull me back into the corridor the second it gets too dangerous, but I hope I can get Silver before it gets bad.

"Taishi's leaning out of the window," he reports. "I think he's asking Willow if he should whistle for Silver."

"NO!" I say, extremely alarmed. "What if he comes to the whistle and jumps out of the window?"

Jack and Piper look horrified at this thought.

"I'll tell them," Piper says quickly, and sprints to their room.

"You want *me* to whistle?" Johnny Two-Legs asks, touching me lightly on the shoulder. "It'll likely be loud," he warns.

I nod and stick my fingers in my ears. "We can just blame it on owls," I tell him, thinking what mam will say if she wakes up and hears a tremendous whistle.

Johnny Two-Legs puts his fingers in his mouth and lets out the loudest, most piercing whistle I've ever heard--four short ones and a long one. I really hope that Silver will hear it straight away. Mam and dad will definitely think something is up if they hear that sound more than once in a night because I don't think owls really sound anything like that. I strain my ears but can't hear anything except the wind. Piper comes dashing back into the corridor, wincing at the noise made by Two-Legs.

"I told the others to call through the window," she says, out of breath. "Hopefully, the pirates on the island will hear them and go in that direction instead." She frowns. "I told them not to be too loud, but after that whistle, I don't think we need to worry."

"But Silver might jump through the window when he hears them!" I say. There is a panicky feeling in my chest. "Piper! Why did you <u>do</u> that?!"

"Oh, I..." she says, and her face looks panicky, too. "Well... surely he'll come to a whistle, rather than someone shouting? I mean, he can't have gone that far... can he?"

The beach is still brightly lit by the moon and the zillions of stars, but the jungle is dark and thick, with small fires burning here and there where the pirates were making camp. Calls, shouts and whistles are from all directions. I hear Taishi and

Willow in the next room, and Two-Legs's breathing, heavy and worried in my ear.

"It sounds like there are lots more than three of them out there," Jack says. His face is stretched forward, as if pointing towards where he is looking - a bit like Silver's. If he could have, I bet he would have pricked up his ears and tilted them to hear better.

"Aye, many more. Looks like they've called for reinforcements," Johnny Two-Legs breathes.

We stand together, very still.

It's awful waiting for something we can't see.

A rush of alarm sweeps over me and I know I have to do something straightaway, or we will all implode. Without saying anything to the others, I jump away from them, ripping myself out of Jack's slack grip on my pyjamas, and leap onto the sand.

"SILVER!" I shout, my voice cracking in desperation.

The sounds from the jungle suddenly seem to point straight towards me like an arrow. Then I hear a thundering sound and Silver appears at the edge of the sand, running as fast as I've ever seen him run. Behind him are shouts.

"A window!" someone yells. "Lads! There's a window! Hanging in the air!"

He sounds astonished - as well he might. I stare back at Jack, framed in the doorway, eyes wide in terror.

"Come on, boy!" I roar at Silver.

Silver leaps at me and tries to lick my face as I put my arms around him and drag him back through the door. I collapse onto the floor, the carpet feeling odd after the sand, and hug him tight. "You stupid dog!" I half-shout, holding him while he wriggles. "Don't do that again!"

Taishi bangs the next-door window shut, and he and Willow join us from the other room. Taishi's face is flushed with relief and I feel sick now I have a second to realise how close we came to being caught and put onto a child-stealing ship.

"Well." Willow heaves a tremendous sigh of relief. "Thank goodness for that. That's the door closed and everyone accounted for. Right?"

"Ye-es," I said, glancing at Jack. "But..."

"But what?" Piper asks dangerously.

"But the pirates have found the window," I blurt.

Jack says a word that even Dad might have frowned at. Johnny Two-Legs raises his eyebrows almost completely to his hat.

"It'll stay open there even if it's closed here, won't it?" I say.

Everyone is quiet for a moment, and then Willow speaks.

"Right. Well, there's only one thing for it. I'm going to sneak back across the island and shut the window."

She puts her hands up as everyone starts protesting at once.

"The window'll disappear as soon as I close it, right?" she says. "And I'm sneakier than all of you. I'll be there and back before you know it." She puts her bag down and moves to the door, shaking off Piper's hand on her arm. "I'm going now before I get too nervous," she says, determinedly. "Wait here for me. But you must close the door if the pirates come, ok?"

And without saying another word, she bursts back through the door and takes off at a run across the sand, leaving us gobsmacked in her wake.

Close The Island Window

Willow

My heart pounds as I race as fast as I can to the cover of the trees. I spy a cluster of bushes clumped around the trunk of a huge palm tree and dive into them to get my bearings. I have to be sure I know where I'm going, but right now I can hear the rush of my pulse in my ears, louder than the sea, and I'm shaking a bit with nerves. I make myself breathe slowly and think hard. I know I can get to the window and back without being seen - the pirates are looking for a noisy dog, not a silent girl - but it will be a disaster if I bump into one by accident. They would probably take me to work in their gold mine - or feed me to the monster that Johnny Two-Legs was talking about. And the others wouldn't know I'd been taken until it was too late! I strain my ears.

"It wasn't that far!"

The voice comes suddenly from my right, far closer than is comfortable. My heart begins to race again. They are so close I can even *smell* them: it's a weird mix of burning oil and sweat. Holding my breath, I peek around the trunk of the tree. There is a scruffy-looking young man, standing behind a tall woman wearing a patched up jacket with a badge stitched onto the shoulder. Her forehead is full of deep wrinkles and her hair has bits of grey, and she has a look on her face as though she's just stepped in Silver's poo (I hope she has). She snaps irritably at the man.

"Lift that torch 'igher, Critchell."

Critchell is holding a burning torch, which he lifts over their heads. It singes a leaf and they both look sharply up, and I quickly crouch to the ground, heart hammering. There's a pause, in which I imagine those dirty faces peering over me, but then I hear them moving away, crashing carelessly through the bushes.

"How many did Danny say 'e'd seen?" the woman asks. "Three young 'uns or four?"

"Don't think 'e said," the man replies. He clears his throat and spits, and then adds, in an oily voice, "That deserter Two-Legs should swing for taking the boy, miss."

"No need for boot-licking, Critchell," the woman snaps. "I'm first mate, not captain. But if you get those other kids, I'll see you get extra rations of grog."

The man gives a creepy chuckle. My stomach turns over and I try to shrink further into the bushes, hoping against hope they don't turn around again.

"If there's any big ones, they'll go to the mine," the first mate says, her voice carrying on the wind with the screech of a seagull. "Any little ones, though, Captain'll just feed 'em to the critter."

Now I feel properly sick. If the first mate is this bad, imagine what Captain Babs will be like? Not to mention her hungry critter. The pirates continue talking loudly as they move away. Clearly, they aren't bothered about being heard--which, when you think about it, is a bit stupid, as they're trying to capture someone. But at least *I* know exactly where *they* are. I wait until they're a little further away and I can breathe easier, then I wipe my sweating palms on my pyjama bottoms and creep slowly towards Taishi and Two-Legs's campsite. I stop there, noticing with interest the smaller hammock (that I assume belongs to Taishi) that we hadn't seen on our first night, and take a deep breath.

My heart is still racing, but I try to think sensibly. When we first went to the clearing, we went along the beach and then down the little path, past Silver's poo. When we came *back* from the clearing, to the door, we came *through* the trees. So

I should be able to reach the window by going through the trees again, as long as I'm careful. The advantages are:

1.I'll be hidden. If I went along the beach, there'd be more chance of being seen.

2. It's a much shorter route. It won't take me as long to get to the window as it would if I went along the beach.

But the disadvantages are:

1.I won't be able to see the pirates until I'm really close to them.

2. I <u>think</u> I can remember the way to the window - but I'm not one hundred percent sure.

I think for a moment, listening hard. The sweat on my back has cooled down, and it's making me feel chilly. I can't hear anything except the wind and the sea, but that doesn't mean that there aren't pirates nearby. I clench my fists for a second in determination, and then step away from the campsite, into the trees.

Once I get going, it's not too hard to find my way. There is a path along sandy grass between thick bushes with rubbery leaves, and I sneak silently from one slab of moonlight to the next, pausing each time to listen hard and smell the air, to see if anyone is close. It only takes a few minutes to reach the glade where the window hangs in the air. I crouch behind a tree and scan the clearing to make sure the pirates haven't left anybody on lookout - and it's a good job I do, because there is a movement on the far side of the clearing and a small figure emerges from the shadows. They stroll casually across the empty space in front of the window; they obviously don't think they're being watched.

How am I going to get to the window without being seen? I desperately scan the area, looking for anything that might give me an idea or offer a distraction.

The pirate reaches the other side of the tiny clearing, stares up at the sky and then yawns widely, pulling something out of their pocket of their long, flared jacket. It's a bottle. They take a long drink and put it back, and then swipe their long hair away from their face. Then they turn and walk across the clearing again. As they enter the moonlight, I see that it's a woman - and not the woman I had seen walking noisily through the jungle earlier. This woman is... *sinister* somehow.

She is the scariest looking woman I have ever seen. I don't know if it's her bony face, or her long, witchy fingers, or the way she leans slightly forward as she walks, as though she's hunting something. Whatever it is, my blood runs cold. This <u>has</u> to be Babs Bembridge. As I watch, she turns around and I freeze. She's small and sinewy and buzzing with a creepy sort of energy I have never felt before. Her face is narrow and her dark eyebrows are drawn together as though she's suspicious of the jungle around her. The look on her face makes me extra glad I'm hidden. She glares at the window and then, with a look on her face as if she's concentrating hard, she stretches her arms out in front of her, sort of like a zombie (only not as funny), and slowly walks back towards the window. From my position close to the jungle floor, it looks as though she is only a pair of legs, her top half made invisible by the magical window. She mutters something angrily, then turns and stamps away across the clearing.

"Jonas! Pedro? Damn it, you scoundrels, how have you not found them yet?" Her voice pierces through the night air, brimming with authority. I hear a small, scuffling shout in the distance, voices replying, and then she disappears from sight back into the trees on the far side of the clearing.

This is my chance.

I scramble up and race across the clearing and around to the front of the window. A blast of wind from Merryshields hits me in the face as I grab the handle and yank the window closed. As soon as the clasp hooks onto the latch, the whole thing vanishes and my hands are suddenly empty. There's no time to dwell on how strange it is, though - it's time for me to go. I dart back into the shadows, moving quickly as I retrace my steps, listening hard for any sounds. I almost trip and tumble into camp in my haste to see the door, but when I look out across the beach, it's nowhere to be seen.

Instead, on the sand, arguing in the starlight, are another two pirates: men this time, one tall and broad, one round-headed and shorter than his companion. They are standing right in the middle, between the camp and where I know the door is - Jack must have had to shut it to avoid being seen. I freeze, waiting anxiously. From behind me, I hear a mad roar that makes the two pirates stop arguing and look towards the sound. Their faces in the moonlight look like mine and Piper's when mum's caught us playing instead of tidying our room - if mum was a child-stealing, monster-owning witch. Then they sprint towards the shouting. I stay where I am, and heave a sigh of relief when, after just a few seconds, the door reappears. It cracks very slightly open, and Piper's terrified face peers around it.

"Here!" I hiss, and sprint towards her. In eight seconds flat, I skid across the threshold and Piper closes the door behind me with shaking hands. "Right," I say breathlessly. "Please tell me everyone who should be here *is* here! I'm not going in there again!"

Piper hugs me, half furious. "I heard the pirates arguing!" she says, on the breath of a sob. "I thought they'd found you!"

I put my arms around her and give her a huge squeeze of relief. "Come on," I say. "Let's get out of here."

We file down the corridor and around a corner, into another one of the attic rooms, where we all collapse onto the floor. Everyone is wide-eyed in shock. Through the window, I see storm clouds lit up by intermittent moonlight, and small spots of rain splatter against the glass. The house seems to shimmer around us, muffling the outside world, and I instinctively feel that we are safe here. The Olds can't hear us, and the pirates can't get to us. I pull my bag open and take charge. (Someone has to.)

"Johnny Two-Legs, please can you light this?" I ask, handing him a huge, heavy candle I'd found in one of the rooms earlier.

"Piper, give these out. Jack, pour this - not now, it's dark, you idiot! Wait a minute."

A few seconds later, Johnny Two-Legs lights the candle and places it in the middle of the floor, where it casts a warm, cosy glow. Now there's light to see by, Jack pours drinks into paper cups and Piper hands everyone a bread roll. I open a plastic tub and pull out a single chicken drumstick for each of us cousins, then give the tub and remaining drumsticks to Two-Legs and Taishi. Two-Legs holds it to his nose like it's the best thing he's ever smelled.

"This is the best thing I've ever smelled," he sighs.

"Thanks for the apple juice, Willow," Piper says.

"Oh! I've got milk!" I say in surprise. "But I filled the bottle with water."

Jack peers into his cup. "Orange juice, for me," he notes.

Two-Legs raises his cup. "Ale."

Taishi sniffs cautiously. "Lemonade?" he asks, curiously.

Kit grins. Even in the dim light from the candle, I can see that his mouth is surrounded by hot chocolate. "Best midnight feast ever," he says.

The Storm

Jack

We decide it's best if Two-Legs and Taishi stay in the attic (which sounds worse than it is). When we finish eating, Kit cries out and points to the corner of the room. The good old house has supplied us with a huge pile of cushions and blankets, so it's as comfortable as any one of our beds, if not more--*and*, it's much less risky than Two-Legs and Taishi staying in a room downstairs where the Olds can find them. Two-Legs is astonished at the appearance of their new bedding, but as Willow points out to him, it's hardly surprising that a house like Merryshields can provide something as simple as blankets when it holds a whole world inside just *one* of its rooms. We wave goodnight, promising to come and see them the next morning and start our journey back to our rooms.

Back in the little family wing, we turn a corner to find Dad standing at the bathroom door looking curiously down the corridor, *right at us!* We freeze and stand still as statues, hearts pounding, convinced we're about to be found out... but after the longest minute ever, he ambles back off to bed and we breathe a collective sigh of relief.

"No glasses," Piper points out, and I realise she's right. Dad can't see a thing when he's not got his glasses on.

"The house is helping us get back to bed without being seen," Kit breathes.

"Really?" Piper yawns. She can be so sarcastic when she's tired.

Kit raises his eyebrows at her. "Yes. Really," he says, indicating the dark windows with a flourish.

Piper stares at him. "What?"

"Can you see anything through these windows?" Piper looks at him blankly and Kit sighs. "Where's the *moon*, Piper?" he hisses.

He usually takes a long time to lose his temper, so I diagnose sleepiness and take charge.

"Upstairs, the moon was lighting up the corridor, in-between the storm clouds, " I explain, taking Kit's shoulder and propelling him towards our bedroom. "Now the storm clouds have covered the sky, the *lightning* should be lighting everything up. But look." I point at another window as we turn a corner. "We can't see anything at all. See?"

She nods her head, agreeing reluctantly, and Willow smiles tiredly behind her back. I glance at the window again. It really is uncanny, once you notice it. All the way from the attic, through every window, I had noticed the moon coming in and out from behind the huge dark storm clouds. The lightning had flashed and lit up the wet grounds of the house outside. But here in the family wing the windows are dark and still, as though nothing particular is going on outside them. I smile as we reach our room, patting the doorframe as I follow Kit inside.

"Thanks, house. Night girls."

Kit and I climb into our beds and dive under the covers. I'm asleep before I can even finish a thought.

We *planned* to visit Two-Legs and Taishi in the attic straight after breakfast this morning, but the Olds put paid to that idea within seconds of us opening our eyes.

"What's going on?" I ask, yawning so widely my jaw cracks. Kit is grumbling across the room as Mam pulls his covers off.

"Didn't you hear the storm?" Mam asks, hustling us out of the room and down to the kitchen as fast as she can. "It was the biggest storm the country's had in years! Trees down all over the place! That big oak out in the front got hit by lightning! It was wild! Mind you," she adds, her eyebrows coming together, "I'm not surprised you slept through it."

She glares at us meaningfully, and I put my head down. I knew she wouldn't forgive and forget that easily. I suppose I wouldn't, either, if she'd vanished for a whole night.

In the kitchen, the pans hanging on the wall gleam comfortingly and fairy lights that Auntie Percy has hung around the Welsh dresser (don't ask me why it's Welsh, Mam says it came from Cornwall) are twinkling in a cheerful fashion. It's like a different room to the one we spent all yesterday cleaning. There's no sign of Dad, but I can hear Auntie Percy in the utility room arguing with the washing machine.

"Did something happen to the house, Aunt Seren?" asks Piper, rubbing her eyes at the kitchen table.

"Did something happen to the house?!" Mam repeats hysterically. "Let's see... four separate floods *that we know of so far,* at least *twelve* windows broken, no guttering left at all and dozens upon dozens of roof tiles off! We need you lot out from under our feet while we decide which bits of the house are still safe!"

She slams two slices of bread into the toaster, which makes me flinch as I pour my cornflakes. Piper scans the kitchen, her eyes narrowed, and I guess she's wondering what we can stash away to take up to Taishi and Johnny Two-Legs. For the first time, I wonder what they're going to do now. For one thing, we are a *long* way from the sea. For another, Two-Legs looks far too pirate-y to fit in in the real world and Taishi would definitely draw attention to himself walking around with no shoes - even now, in summer. So they are going to have to go into the actual world sooner or later. Unless...

Auntie Percy comes in from the utility room with a basket full of soaking wet washing. "That washing machine isn't spinning all the water out," she sighs. "It's almost not worth hanging this lot out on the line, the way the weather looks." She notices me staring into nothingness as I consider the Two-Legs and Taishi conundrum, and frowns. "Are you alright, Jack, love?" she asks. "It's not like you to sit in a dream."

"I'm fine," I tell her, smiling. I think it will be quite fun to have a pirate living in the house. I bet he's got loads of stories to tell.

Dad appears through the back door, knocking into Auntie Percy as she plonks her basket down. "Sorry," he says gruffly, looking harassed. "Right, you lot." He looks at us and I see the glint of tyranny in his eyes. He has assumed a captain's role and is on a mission. I can feel our plans slipping away, and my stomach sinks in disappointment. "I've got a job for you," he continues. "I need you to count all the windows in the house, and then-" he holds up a hand to stop us interrupting, "-then, I need you to count how many are broken. We never got a final answer on the window count from the estate agents - it's almost as though every time they counted them, there were a different number - and we'll need to know if we're going to replace any of them, so you may as well make yourselves useful." He smiles thinly, but he definitely doesn't have the usual Dad twinkle.

Kit and I look at each other.

"Dad, can I just run up and get something from my room?" Kit asks.

I inwardly sigh. There's no way he would have enough time to get all the way up to the attic and back without arousing suspicion.

"Of course you can!" Mam says, surprising us.

Kit gives me a meaningful wink, and I know he wants me to cause a distraction, so he's got time to sprint all the way to the attic and back. Piper begins sliding a box of cereal across the table towards him. We can't take a proper breakfast, but cornflakes are better than nothing.

"We'll come with you," Auntie Percy smiles, patting my shoulder. "That washing can wait a minute." My heart sinks and so does Kit's face. He slumps back into his chair and Piper sighs and pours herself more cornflakes, instead. "Your mum and I want to check the state of your windows, anyway," Auntie Percy is explaining. "Hang on while I get another coffee."

She hurries away to the kettle and the four of us exchange glances. Not only can we not get up to the attic to see Johnny Two-Legs and Taishi, we have to spend the day counting windows. Things are going from annoying to infuriating.

Half an hour later, we are out in the cold, damp spring, with raincoats, clipboards, and grumpy expressions. Dad has walked us to the side of the house that we haven't been to yet, opposite where our family wing is. I remind the crew under my breath that Johnny Two-Legs told us not to worry about them. Piper frowns at the grey sky. "It had better not rain."

"Oh, it's going to!" Dad says cheerfully - and as though he's commanded it, it does. He seems a lot chirpier suddenly, now that we're outside. "Come on. Let me give you your instructions."

We listen, clutching the clipboards to our chests as the rain falls heavily and dad tells us how to count, where to count, what to count, and all manner of other counting-related things to note that we don't care about. He doesn't seem to be at all bothered about the drips hanging off his nose and spattering his glasses.

"Got it?" he asks.

We all nod.

"Good." He looks up at the house again. "Lucky for you," he says, with a slight grimace, "some good came from your overnight escapade. The farmer's son-in-law is a roofer who's happy to get some cash-in-hand work." He sighs at the massive leaking building. "It'll take all our cash," he mutters, "but at least we'll be dry while we're starving."

He smiles as he waves and walks away, but I catch the serious look in his eyes and it makes my stomach churn uncomfortably. I wait until he's back on the gravel path and then turn to the others.

"We *have* to find that treasure," I say.

"'Course we do," Piper says.

"No, I mean it," I say. "It's desperate. It's got to be our complete priority."

"After counting all these windows, you mean," Kit moans. "Don't look at me like that, you know I'm right. They'll *never* trust us again if we don't do as we're told now."

Willow looks at him in admiration. "Kit, it's almost like you've been *listening* to the Olds!" she gasps, winking. He grins. I only just stop myself stamping my foot in frustration.

"Guys, this is real! I'm serious!" I grit my teeth. "Look, you heard our dad: there won't be any money left after they fix the roof. That means they can't finish the holiday cottages, which means no money can come from people staying here. Not to mention that no-one can have holidays with lockdown now anyway! All their money is going into the house, you've heard them say it as often as I have. And if they have to choose between the house and feeding us..."

They look at me like I'm stupid. I can't believe they haven't thought of this already.

"We'll. Have. To. Leave," I say, very slowly, so that they understand. "It's the best place we've ever been, and we won't be able to stay if we can't help them find the money to keep going."

"The treasure must be on the island!" Kit bursts out. "It's on the map, and the island is on the map, and there are pirates on the island, so there *must* be the treasure there, too!"

I can't fault his logic - I mean, the house <u>did</u> show us Silver and the orchard, too, but... "It's not that straightforward," I tell him. "I mean, for one thing, we don't know for sure that the treasure *is* on the island."

"And for another, we are absolutely *not* going back to check!" Piper interjects firmly. "We'll just have to look some-where else in the house."

"Maybe the map can give us another clue," Willow says. Kit looks hopeful and I shake my head at him. I don't want him to get his hopes up.

"Maybe," I say, "but I looked at it when Dad and I went to pick up the pencils, and there's nothing else there. Piper's right; we can't risk going back to the island. But we have to do *something*. We can't leave Merryshields. We just can't."

My heart is sinking further and further down each time I think about it. The situation just seems hopeless.

"Do you really think it's that serious?" Kit asks quietly.

I nod. "There's no money coming in anymore, not since Dad lost his job, and mam said she may as well pay her salary straight to the supermarket, and Auntie Percy..." I stop, because I know Auntie Percy gave up her job when Uncle Toby went to New York, and I heard her telling our mam that she felt awful about not paying her way. "Well, anyway, all of their savings went on buying the house. So-"

"If there's no money, what happens?" Willow is as practical as always.

Piper tugs on her plait. "I heard Mum talking to Dad on the phone yesterday, when I went to ask her about the sandwiches," she says. "He said that, if necessary, we could go and live with Gran." The sisters look at each other. "Obviously I couldn't hear him," Piper admits, "but I guessed that's what he said. He thinks Mum can't look after us with no money, and he always said he didn't want his money eaten by this house."

It's exactly the kind of thing I can imagine Uncle Toby saying. If he was here, things would be a lot more energetic - he's very 'solution-orientated' is how Willow puts it, and Piper eyes her sideways, which is her way of agreeing without wanting to show it. Uncle Toby likes to get things done, and if something's not working, he moves right on until he finds something that will. Which is kind of what I heard Mam saying to Auntie Percy one night before we moved. That Uncle Toby thought their marriage wasn't working, so he was moving right on... I didn't want to hear the rest of the conversation so I stopped listening. The point is, if his money was going to be eaten by something, Uncle Toby would want it to be worth it.

We all look up at Merryshields. I don't know much about buildings eating money, but anyone can see that this one is enormous, so the bills must be enormous too.

I swallow. "There's nothing else we can do to help," I say into the silence. "But if we can stay out of trouble and finish counting these windows, then at least we can go *looking* for the treasure. I think Merryshields must have it hidden somewhere else. It's just a question of where."

We're quiet for a moment before Piper clears her throat. "Someone's got to say it," she says, "and I wish I didn't have to, but... what if there isn't any treasure?"

The rain falls noisily in the leaves above us and fat drops drip onto my forehead.

There's a line between Willow's brows. "There are other things on the pictures the aren't real," she says. "Like that door in Headquarters that isn't there. So maybe..." She swallows. "Maybe Piper's right. Maybe there isn't any treasure."

"There has to be," I say fiercely. "Think of the *other* pictures on the map! It wouldn't show Silver, or the orchard, or the key, all being real, and make the treasure just a picture."

We all watch Silver galloping delightedly through the wet grass. He is definitely a very real dog, and just a few days ago he was nothing more than a picture and an ornament. I refuse to believe that after all of this, Merryshields wouldn't help us when we need it most.

"Come on," I say roughly. "Let's get started."

Counting Windows

Piper

W e are a miserable little group. The more I look at the blank window panes, the emptier they seem, and the island behind the door seems more impossible than ever. If it wasn't for the sunburn on the back of my neck, I would think it was all a dream.

Jack is right about the state of things. I absolutely do <u>not</u> want to live at Gran's. For one thing, the four of us love being together, and for another, as much as me and Willow love Gran, her house isn't magical. Can you imagine what it'd be like if Jack and Kit got to explore the whole house and discover everything without us? Or worse - if they had to leave, too, and that was the end of the magic altogether?

I count the windows without noticing the numbers, trying to remember every little magical thing the house has done. Jack is right about the map showing pictures that have come true, but it's a lot easier to be hopeful when we're exploring than when we're standing out in the cold rain, with the possibility of living at Gran's house hanging over our heads. I try not to think about the picture of the Headquarters door-that-isn't-there.

"How many have you got?" Willow asked.

"Um... I think I got up to 78?" I say.

She shakes her head in confusion. "We all got different numbers. I counted three times and got a different number every time! This is going to take forever!"

Kit looks up towards the attic. "I hope Taishi and Johnny Two-Legs are alright," he says worriedly.

"They'll have seen worse storms than this," Jack says. "And this time, they were under a proper roof."

"Even if it leaked," Kit agrees. "You're right. I just can't believe we haven't been able to go up there and see them. Stupid storm." He stamps in a puddle and water splashes everywhere.

"Kit!" I say, gently.

"What? You're already soaking!" he points out. Which is fair, I suppose. But still, I don't really want to get any wetter than I have to.

"Come on," Willow says, shaking a raindrop off her nose. "If we hurry up, we'll be allowed back in again, and we can get a picnic to go and see them. I bet Mrs Boudry will give us a big feast, since we've been so helpful."

"You really think that's how it works?" I ask.

"Of course," she says.

I'm not so sure, although I can see the logic. After all, when we were stuck on that island all night, the house was cross with us and messed up the kitchen. Then we tidied and it gave us some fruit. And when we went to rescue Two-Legs and Taishi, it gave us roast chicken. So maybe Willow's right.

"Fingers crossed." My tummy gives a huge rumble as I say this and the others giggle. "Let's be as quick as we can," I mutter, "or it really will take us forever."

Merryshields has so many walls and nooks and outbuildings and courtyards that it's lunchtime by the time we get all the way around. The wind is whipping wildly around every corner when we finally start down the west side.

"Last side!" Jack says bracingly. "Well, sort of."

"We've got to go all round the family wing first," Willow complains.

"I'm going to have a house with *no* windows when I grow up," Kit grumbles. "This is the most boring thing I've ever done."

Last year's leaves are twirling in the corner where the Family Wing meets the main house. I tuck my chin into my jacket and clutch the clipboard close to my chest. When we work our way round the other side, the wind is even stronger and we all look up at the roof in concern.

"Do you think it'll fall down?" Kit asks.

"No," I say firmly, although I'm not altogether certain.

"Do you think Johnny Two-Legs and Taishi got any sleep?" Willow asks. "Our window was rattling all night. It must have been so noisy up there."

"Look," says Jack. "The kitchen window's open. Shall we just see if there's any food on the go? I can't believe we haven't had any lunch!"

Happy to have a reason to go inside for a minute, we all troop to the kitchen, leaving soggy footprints in our wake. There's no sign of Mrs Boudry and we are sent back outside almost immediately by Mum. Worry is making her face tight and shiny, but she does at least load us up with biscuits and a flask of weak, warm tea. We count the rest of the West Wing windows and then, with big sighs of relief, move at last to the front of the house.

"Systems begin," Jack orders.

Since he developed the system of counting that has proven to be most effective, we let him be captain of counting. He sends Kit scampering across the gravel towards the house, almost falling into the overgrown flowerbeds as Silver barrels into him from behind. Willow and I then count the ground floor windows out loud as Kit slowly walks past them, covering the width of the house and back again so we can double-check the count. We report the number to Jack, who records it on his clipboard, and then Willow takes Kit's place. We repeat the method as we count the first floor. I do the walking for the second floor and Kit takes his place again as we reach the attic. We are trying not to rush, feeling relieved that we have almost finished, when Willow moans and puts her hands over her mouth, her eyes wide above them.

"What is it?" I ask in alarm.

"Are you going to throw up?" Jack asks, taking a cautious step back.

Willow shakes her head and points, and I crane my neck to see.

"What the... what?!"

Kit, who is making his way slowly back across the building for our second-check and final count of the attic windows lets out a shout. He's seen it, too. He sprints across the grass, sliding into a damp heap at our feet.

"The window! The window!" he cries, too out of breath to say more. But by this point, we've all seen it.

The window of the island room, which Willow had closed so determinedly in the middle of the night, is wide open and swinging on its hinges. We look at each other, horrified.

"Surely the pirates would have sailed off the island once they realised nobody was there?" There is a tremble in Willow's voice.

"Surely the window was closed long enough that they would have just left?" I say. "Maybe it's only just now blown open?"

Jack shakes his head doubtfully. "All of that guttering you were using to hold onto yesterday while you climbed back in to the next room is gone. If the wind was strong enough to rip the guttering off the roof, it must have been strong enough to re-open that window," he says grimly. He's right; the guttering is in pieces all over the lawn where the wind has scattered it.

"But that means even if someone has noticed that the window is open again, they wouldn't be able to climb out," I say reassuringly. "Really, it's no different to how it was before."

I am cool and calm on the outside, but on the inside my heart is pounding three times faster than normal. What if the wind has blown the door open, too? In a normal room, that's how it would work, but I have no idea if it would work the same way when there's a whole island *between* the window and the door inside.

"We have company," Willow mutters, nodding at Mum, who is walking across the lawn towards us.

"This is a lovely tree you're sheltering under," she says cheerfully. "Did you like the biscuits? We thought you might have had enough by now, so I came out to see how you're getting on."

"We think we've counted right, Auntie Percy," Kit says. Jack holds up his clipboard with all the counts written down. "It's taken ages, though. Did you fix the leaks?"

"Not yet," she says. "But we've contained them, so that's a good start. Why do you all look so worried?" She turns and peers up at the top of the house. "Oh, that window!" she says. "The latches in those attic rooms are so temperamental! And you wouldn't believe the amount of rain that's come in overnight. There's half an ocean of it!" She squeezes my shoulder. "Don't worry, lovey. It'll get fixed. We're not giving up on this house just yet. Let's get you all inside."

We follow her back towards the house.

"Will we really be staying, Auntie Percy?" Jack asks.

Mum stops and looks at us all seriously. "I want to say yes," she sighs, "but the way things are at the moment, I can't promise anything. This house has already stretched our budget tighter than we thought it would, and we really don't have any more savings to fall back on." She wipes her wet hair out of her face. "We already had some bookings for that one holiday cottage, which would have given us a bit of a buffer. But circumstances being what they are with lockdown..." She trails off, her gaze looking unfocussed for a moment before she draws herself upright with a visible effort. "And this whole thing with Great-Auntie Glynis-"

"What _is_ the thing with Great-Auntie Glynis?" Kit interrupts. "She's like a thousand years old and lives in that cabbagey home with the old man who always shouts at us to be quiet even though he can't hear anything."

"No," Jack says, elbowing him. "That's Auntie _Doris_. Glynis Goodwin is the one who smells of wee."

"Jack! It's _Auntie_ Glynis," Mum says, but she's smiling. "But yes, she does smell a bit, poor thing."

"She _told_ us to call her Glynis Goodwin," Jack says.

"Well, she's probably forgotten about that now," Mum says. "She's forgetting all sorts of things. Last week, the carer spent four hours searching for her purse only to find it in the freezer. And if things get worse, we might have to..." She glances back at the house and I'm sure I see a tear run down her face, mixing with the rain. "... if it gets worse, we might have to leave Merryshields," she finishes, and gives a little sniff.

Our mouths open in shock.

"Yes, I thought you might be pleased," Mum says miserably, totally misinterpreting our looks. "It means we'll be in a smaller house - probably one of those new builds on the other side of the hill, with a little granny annex where we can keep an eye on Glynis - but we'll be closer to your friends and the shops again. You won't have a garden as big as this, but-"

"Those houses are tiny!" Willow splutters.

"Dad said their gardens are the size of postage stamps!" Jack says, sounding horrified. "He said it the last time we drove past, before we got here. He said we were lucky we didn't all have to live cramped up in one of those boxes!"

Mum holds her hands up to stop us. "Look, all of you! Look on the bright side! If we have to move, we might be able to spend more time together, and you wouldn't have loads of angry grown-ups ignoring you all the time. You might even get to go back to school!" She wipes her eyes with her wrist, and we look at each other in growing consternation. "If Aunt Seren and I have to go back to work, and your Dad-" she looks at the boys, "-gets a job driving a delivery van, then you might be classed as children of key workers. You know, those are the kids that can go to school during this whole pandemic."

I can't think of anything to say. The others shuffle around, looking at the ground.

Mum smiles sadly at us. "We're not there just yet," she says. "Where there's a will there's a way, and we're trying our best to hold everything together." She takes a step towards the house and then stops again with a stern expression. "But no more night-time wanderings! Alright?!"

We laugh sheepishly and continue walking, but I see Kit grab Jack beside me and the two of them stop dead. When I follow their glance, I see the unmistakable outline of a person at the open attic window - and they are holding a rope.

Who Doesn't Want Cinema Night?

Kit

For once, the Olds want to spend time with us. Maybe it's because of the night we went missing, or maybe it's because we spent all day out in the rain counting windows for them, or maybe Auntie Percy reported how upset we'd been at the thought of leaving Merryshields and moving into a tiny little house with a smelly old lady, but it's obvious they've had a conversation and decided that we all need to spend some family time together. Which would have been fun a week ago, but now that we've got so much to do, it's a bit awkward having them hanging around.

Us cousins grab a chance to talk to each other while the Olds are busy getting food for an indoor picnic and finding the moving box with the board games in (luckily, that box had been in our car so it didn't end up in the river with the removal van). We huddle together in the kitchen, making sandwiches and talking in quiet voices.

"How on earth are we going to get out of this?" Jack asks quietly.

Piper and Willow look at each other.

"There's nothing we can do," Willow says. "You've seen that look in their eyes before."

I hate to admit it, but they're right. Our mam and Auntie Percy aren't the same in everything (even though they are sisters), but one thing they *do* have in common is this one particular expression. It's determination, mixed with excitement, mixed with perseverance, mixed with love - and some more determination sprinkled on top. Usually, you only see it at times like on sports day, when they get competitive, or maybe on holidays, when they want it to be the best holiday ever so they pull out all the stops. So usually that expression on their faces is a good thing for all of us. But today it means hours and hours of their devoted attention when we *really* don't have the time.

All I can think about is making sure Johnny Two-Legs and Taishi get some food. We also *really* need to talk about the whole pirate-at-the-window problem. AND, we still have to find the treasure. We need some time to look at the scrapbook and see if the house has given us any more clues.

It is the longest afternoon in the history of afternoons. We play Monopoly for hours and we can't lose even though we really try to. We eat until we're stuffed (I can't complain about that). Then we watch a film, which normally would have been great - I even get to sit between my mam and my dad, though I nearly get evicted for fidgeting. When we're finally set free, it's bedtime, and none of us dare to sneak out for the third night in a row, so we decide to wait until morning.

Thankfully, when we go downstairs for breakfast, we find the Olds have gone back to normal - in other words, grumpy and wanting us out of their hair. Willow stuffs her bag with all the food she can manage whenever the Olds turn their backs or look away for a second - she's like a ninja! Silver sniffs at her bag interestedly, and she pushes him gently away. This food is for Two-Legs and Taishi. As soon as we can, we leave the kitchen. First, we walk calmly and then, when we get to the stairs, we break out into a run and race for the attic.

"We should stop here," Piper pants, when we reach the last door between us and the attic corridor.

"Why?" Jack asks impatiently.

"To see if we can hear anyone?" Piper replies with maximum sarcasm.

We hold our breath and listen at the door. I can smell the sea, but I can't hear anything moving. Jack opens the door.

The landing is empty.

We sneak along it, trying to keep our footsteps soft and our breathing as quiet as possible.

The room next to the island room (the one where Piper had climbed in through) is empty too, but we can see big damp patches where the rain had seeped in through the window during the storm. I wonder if this is what Mam saw when she opened the island room door, too - it's strange to think that the Olds only see an ordinary house, and not any of the magic of Merryshields at all.

"That window's still shut," Piper whispers. "So, unless the pirates climbed in and closed it after them - which I very much doubt - they haven't come in yet."

We carry on along the corridor. At the Island Room door, we pause again to listen. I put my fingers through Silver's collar even though we aren't going to open it.

"Nothing," says Jack, who is pressing his ear against the wood.

Willow shakes her head. "I *want* to believe that they just sailed away," she says, "but it seems too good to be true. So where could they possibly have gone?"

Feeling uneasy, we creep on round the corner and past two doors, until we come to the little attic room where we'd left Johnny Two-Legs and Taishi.

Piper knocks gently on the door. "It's us," she hisses. "Are you there?"

She opens the door and we peer inside. All the cushions are piled up in the corner again, a bright tumble of colour even though the light from the window is grey. Johnny Two-Legs is sitting on a little three-legged stool, carving something out of a piece of wood, and his parrots are lined up in a row beside him, exactly as though they are watching. His teeth glint cheerfully through his thick black beard. Taishi jumps down from the window, leaving handmarks on the glass behind him, and gives us a huge grin.

"We were wondering when you'd come back!" he cries. "Beginning to get cabin fever, we were."

"S'lovely to see you, mateys," Johnny Two-Legs says

"We're so sorry we couldn't come until now," I say. "It was the storm."

Johnny Two-Legs puts his hand up to stop me. "Never you worry about it," he says firmly. "It was quite a storm, but we've lived through worse."

"At sea, no less," Taishi adds. "It was fun, watching a storm from behind a window in a house instead of through a port-hole in a room that's swishing from side to side."

Willow pulls a scarlet cushion out from the stack and plonks herself down on it. She opens her bag and delves inside. "We brought you some food," she says.

Taishi sits cross-legged beside her, looking expectant, and I sit on her other side.

I clear my throat. Jack waves at me to go on. "We... think there's a problem," I say.

Johnny Two-Legs nods. "I think I know exactly what you are referring to, my lad," he says, gravely. "And I don't think I'm wrong in saying that we haven't much time." He glances at Jack and Piper, who are murmuring together by the door. "Sit you down," he says to them. "We have a few minutes, at least. I think there's time to tell you the full story of how I came to be on the island, and who Babs Bembridge really is."

Two-Legs's Story

Willow

Johnny Two-Legs puts down his knife and the block of wood he's working on, and we all sit down. Me, Jack and Kit are all too anxious to eat - not to mention still full from breakfast and yesterday's feast - but Johnny Two-Legs, Taishi and Piper all dive into the food. Mum thinks Piper must be growing, since she's like a bottomless pit when it comes to food, but I'm not surprised that Two-Legs and Taishi are starving. Even on the island they got to eat fish and coconuts, but in the last twenty-four hours they haven't had anything at all.

Jack is looking at the door.

"What makes you so sure there's time?" he asks. "We saw someone at the window with a rope, and that was *yesterday*."

"Good question," Johnny Two-Legs says, nodding seriously. "That night of the storm, the window in this very room flew wide open and my first thought was of *that* window. But with all the hoo-ha out there - people running up and down, talking about leaks - I didn't dare show my face. I waited until it was quiet, and then I crept along to that room next door to my old island, hung my head out of the window, and listened."

Kit's eyes are wide, one hand holding Silver back, who is trying to put his nose into my bag. I pull it closer to me and dig out a little piece of ham and gave it to him. He inhales it and stares at me lovingly, his tail brushing back and forth across the dusty floor.

"What did you hear?" Kit asks.

"Not a lot! The wind whipped the sounds away before I could make them all out, but I heard enough to know what was happening. Two things in particular, I heard." Two-Legs sighs heavily. "I *wish* I'd been wrong about that ship. I'd hoped to never hear the name Bembridge again, but it's too late for wishes now. But what I did hear..."

He leans forward, and we all hold our breath.

"*Treasure.*"

He leans back, nodding his head slowly, his dark eyes glistening. A cold breeze blows through the gaps in the window, making us all shiver. The three scarlet parrots huddle together, making funny little grumbly noises.

"Treasure?" Jack repeats, a cautious thread of excitement running through his voice.

"Treasure," Taishi confirms, wiping his hands down the front of his shirt. "Here - wherever here is. Babs sensed it, through the window."

"I knew it!" Kit shouts delightedly. "I *knew* the map was right! I knew Merryshields wouldn't let us down!"

Johnny Two-Legs and Taishi look understandably confused at this, so while they finish the packet of gingerbread biscuits, Jack and I give a quick rundown of Merryshields and its magic, starting with the map and Silver, and ending with the Olds, the roof and smelly Great-Aunt-Glynis.

"This map," Johnny Two-Legs says, gathering crumbs fastidiously into the palm of his hand, then scattering them carefully by his feet for the parrots to eat. "You say it shows you that there's treasure?"

"Well..." Piper begins, but Kit interrupts her.

"Yes!" he says firmly. "Did you bring it, Willow? We'll show you!"

I shake my head regretfully. "No! I left it in Headquarters. But it wouldn't help anyone, anyway. It only shows that there <u>is</u> treasure." I don't meet Piper's eye - she's obviously still worried that the treasure might not exist. "It doesn't tell us *where*."

I would have thought that this was a good thing - after all, if *we* can't find the treasure, then surely nobody else would be able to. But something occurs to Piper. Her eyes go wide, even though her mouth is full of biscuit, and she wiggles her fingers at me. Of course. I had forgotten about Babs and her witchy fingers.

Taishi puts down the rope he's fiddling with and looks at us all seriously.

"I can tell you for nothing that she'll find that treasure, come hell or high water. I don't know how we'll do it, but we can't let her in. We *have* to find a way of stopping her. I'm not going back on that ship again. I'd rather die." Taishi looks pale and ill, with huge bags under his eyes as though he hasn't been sleeping well. I take out an apple and hand it to him, not really knowing what else I can do to make him feel better. Two-Legs looks grave.

"We thought we were safe, once we were off that island," he says. "But Babs showing up at that window..."

"So how *do* you know that we've got time before she comes through?" Jack presses. He is fidgeting and keeps looking at the door, and I have to stop myself from going to the corridor to check.

"Now that she knows there's treasure here to be found, she won't rush," Johnny Two-Legs says. "She'll come soon, mark my words, but she won't risk something going wrong for lack of planning. That storm was strong enough to hold them off for a while, but I heard the first mate say that by eight bells today, they'd be through."

"What's eight bells?" asks Kit.

"Noon," Taishi says, looking out of the window. "Johnny's right - there is time. But not much."

"Tell us your story," Jack says, after another glance at the door. "If you're sure there's time."

"Hopefully it'll help us think of what to do," Piper says.

Johnny Two-Legs nods solemnly and begins to tell his tale.

"I first set sail on the ocean blue many years ago, when I was just a lad. I've been all over the world, to places I didn't even know existed--oh, you wouldn't believe some of the wonders I've seen. Everywhere I went, the name of Babs Bembridge was one that nobody wanted to say aloud. People spoke it in whispers, and if they told you a story about her, they looked over their shoulder first and after, to be sure she wasn't there. Rumours flew and swirled wherever she'd been. They said she was responsible for the child snatchings in the villages, and every time treasure of any kind went missing, from the tiniest golden hoop to the most priceless king's crown, 'er name was top of the list. The horrors that went with it - the things she did to people, to get her hands on treasures - it would curdle your soul." He shudders, his eyes focussing on something we can't see.

Taishi nods gravely. "Even I'd heard of her. I was just a ship boy round our local bay, on the fishing boats."

"He's a grand fisherman," Two-Legs beams.

"But whenever the bigger ships came sailing by, the captain would send all of us young 'uns down the hatch to be hidden away, just in case. When we went ashore, the warnings were up on the streets. My mother used to read out the headlines: 'Bembridge's Pirate Thugs Take Mayor's Gold Chain' or 'Five Children Taken Overnight From Palm River School'. It was awful."

"Everyone knew that crew'd do anything to get what they wanted. Buildings burned to ashes, shops looted, men and women harmed for protecting their kids..."

I feel sick. Even Jack looks drained of colour, and Kit has both his arms wrapped tight around Silver. Piper is chewing on her lip and tugging her hair.

Johnny Two-Legs continues. "I last went ashore the year I got married to my sweet Elsie. Now she was a girl to get you talking - I'd sing from the top of the rooftops for her, and I'll tell you, I'm no singer!"

"Prettiest girl in port," Taishi says, making his voice sound deep like Two-Legs's so that we all laugh, despite the conversation. "And the finest cook of them all!"

"I might have told young Taishi here about her, once or twice," Johnny Two-Legs says, smiling. "S'true, though. You'd scrub decks for just a smell of her savoury mince pies, and if you ate a slice of her Caribbean Black fruitcake - tastes of rum and burnt sugar and sunshine - you'd think you were in heaven.

We were strapped for cash, seafarin' not having provided me with much in the way of savings, so I left her with her sister and enlisted on the first merchant ship I could. Didn't think I'd be away long." Two-Legs puts his hat on the floor between us all and begins to twist it slowly around. I feel all the hairs rise along my arms, and Jack rubs hard at the back of his neck, obviously feeling the same prickly sensation.

"They say Babs Bembridge can hear the words spoken on another ship a thousand miles away if the winds are right. I can't say that's true or it's not, but there's no doubt in my mind she's a witch. And not one of them that helps the old and feeds the sick and tells you when to plant your herbs according to the moon." He shakes his head, his long hair swinging. "Babs Bembridge knows things a person oughtn't to know, and she can dowse for gold the way some witches can dowse for water." Johnny Two-Legs's voice is getting softer now. "Both valuable, in their way, but one saves lives and the other makes power. You know what dowsing is?"

Piper raises her hand a little, shyly. "Is it where people use sticks to find water underground?"

Johnny Two-Legs nods. "That's right," he says, gruffly. "Only Babs just needs to stretch out her hands and she feels the vibrations through her fingers. And of course, it's not just the gold *underground*. It's everywhere. In the banks. In the jewellers. In your ears." He gestures at Piper's tiny gold studs and she puts her hands up to them convulsively.

I clap a hand to my mouth. "I *knew* I saw her! On the island! Just before I closed the window - she was standing beside it with her hands out!"

Two-Legs's face scrunches up with worry. "Some say that's what sent her mad: sensing gold everywhere and never being able to escape the vibrations, always feeling the murmuring of the metal against her skin. That's why she took to the seas, they say, where she can ignore the petty metals around her in things like jewellery and small coins, and concentrate instead on the hidden bounties of foreign places and merchant ships."

Taishi frowns. "But that can't be right. I mean, witches who dowse for water live with the sensations all the time, and they manage alright, don't they? The one in our village used to tell us where to build wells or when to barricade our homes for a big storm was coming - she didn't go crazy and she was nice as pie."

Taishi looks at us expectantly and it takes me a moment to understand that he's waiting for us to chip in with our own story.

"Um, we don't know any witches," I say apologetically.

He raises both hands in surprise. "What?! But how would you know where to build a village and dig a well? How do you find your way on long journeys without getting dehydrated? How-"

"-That's not really how it works in our world," Piper cuts in hurriedly.

Taishi exhales in disbelief and shares a look with Two-Legs that shows they think we are far behind the times. It's hard to explain what 'science' is, though I'm sure Jack would love to try. I can see him about to launch into a full explanation and shoot him a look - we don't have the time right now.

Two-Legs tears open a bread roll and shoves a lump of cheese inside it.

"What was the other noise you heard?" Jack asks. "You said you heard two things when you leaned out the window to listen."

Johnny Two-Legs chews slowly and swallows. "The other noise I heard - piercing it was - was a whistle. Not just a *single* whistle, mind. Three long bursts and a short one. It was a signal."

"A signal to who?" Kit whispers.

Johnny Two-Legs whispers back. "Bembridge's ship, *The Roasted Nut.* It was waiting beyond the reef, last we saw of it. I heard that signal many a time when I was part of Bembridge's fleet. The signal lets those still on board the ship know that something has been found on land. The crew would be waiting for them to row back to the *Nut* and be preparing supplies and packs to send out a bigger search party the next day."

"By 'the next day', you mean today," Taishi points out.

I shiver. It starts at the top of my head and ripples all the way down my spine. *Eight bells*, I think.

"What will happen next?" Piper asks in a small, tight voice. "At eight bells?"

Two-Legs looks at her. "Then, I'm afraid to say, she'll come through that window, one way or the other, and go searching until she finds the gold she's sensed from the other side. She'll want to take it, no matter what."

"Nothing stops Babs Bembridge when she puts her mind to something," says Taishi bitterly.

We all go quiet, trying to think of what gold things our family has.

"But we don't <u>have</u> any gold!" Kit finally bursts. "Mam's got some jewellery and her wedding ring, I think..." His voice had the smallest tremor in it. "Would she take that? Mammy would be so sad if she lost it."

Jack looks scared. "The witch would have to take it right off Mam's finger..."

Johnny Two-Legs stares at the boys for a long minute. At first, I think he's trying to come up with a kind way of saying that yes, Babs Bembridge definitely *would* steal Aunt Seren's precious jewellery, but he surprises me by shaking his head. He speaks slowly and carefully.

"I don't believe so...Although I can't promise now, mateys, you see? The thing is, Babs'll have her fingers out for something more substantial than baubles and trinkets. The more exciting a treasure she brings back, the more power she can wield. It increases her powers. She can control the weather, bring storms to the seas, break apart buildings if she needs to... I saw her once direct the lightning at Danny - 'e's never been the same since. And her buccaneers are cruel, vicious men, even being afraid of her - they'll follow wherever she leads, no question." He stops and looks around at us. "I'm afraid of her, and that's the truth."

Piper twiddles her lucky holiday-pirate coin. "But there's nothing *here*. If there was any treasure, we would have used it by now to mend the sodding roof." She flings her hand over her mouth and speaks through it, muffled. "Sorry."

I giggle, despite the heaviness of the conversation. I've never heard Piper swear before. One of the parrots flies up and lands on Piper's shoulder.

"Don't you copy that!" she says. Its beady eyes glint at her, but it only makes a little squawk.

"You're right though, Piper," Jack says. Piper looks at him in shock. "About the roof thing, I mean. If there was anything here, the Olds would have sold it by now to make all the repairs. Not to mention the money for Great Great Stinky Aunt Glynis's downstairs bathroom."

"Then she'd be living with us," Kit grimaces. He sounds as though he'd rather face a pirate witch any day than live with Great Great Aunt Glynis.

"That's true," I say. "*And* they'd be using it to fix up a holiday cottage for Dad. If there was anything valuable here, they wouldn't have to consider us leaving Merryshields just because of a storm."

The four of us breathe a sigh of relief. Even Taishi looks more cheerful.

"She'll only come through if she thinks it's worth it, right Johnny?" he asks hopefully.

Johnny Two-Legs opens his mouth to speak, but Kit interrupts him, patting Silver anxiously. "What about any treasure the house is hiding? *We* need that!"

"Aye, but if this house has any significant treasure, Babs Bembridge'll find it, lad," Johnny Two-Legs says grimly. "If your mapbook tells you there's treasure hidden somewhere in this house, make no mistake - Babs'll put her fingers on it. Only thing to do is find it first, and get it to somewhere she can't find it."

"We have to tell the Olds," Kit says. Jack shakes his head vehemently.

"That's the last thing we should do! We don't know why they don't see any of the Merryshields magic, but we can't risk this being the thing that changes everything! If that witch comes close to Mam, we don't know for certain that she'll be safe! We have to draw the pirates away..."

A loud, piercing whistle echoes along the corridor and my heart is immediately in my throat. We all jump up, Johnny Two-Legs still clutching his sandwich. The birds flutter away to the back of the room.

"Time for talking's over, mateys."

"They've got in," Taishi says, his eyes fixed on the door. "They came through quicker than we thought they would, Johnny. We're too late."

Johnny claps his hand on Taishi's shoulder and gives his sandwich to Silver. "Never give up, boy. It's time for action."

The Pirates Are In

Jack

I put my ear to the door and concentrate all my senses on what's going on.

"What are we going to do?" Willow hisses. "We can't let a witch into the house!"

"She's already in," Piper says. "Or *someone* is, anyway."

"Oh, it'll be her alright. And she won't be alone," Johnny Two-Legs says.

As if on cue, a huge clattering and thumping noise vibrates through the door. Loud, rough voices and the sound of metal and heavy footsteps coming closer. I step back from the door to where the others are standing huddled together, staring at it.

"All the buccaneers," Two-Legs says. He's pulled his long hair back and fastened it at the base of his neck with a piece of string, as though he's preparing for action.

"She'll sense us in here," Taishi says. "She'll know we're here. She'll sense Johnny's earrings." He is trembling. He's pretty tough, so the sight of him so scared makes my skin shiver.

"The house will protect us," Kit says, looking as scared as Taishi beside him. "I'm sure it will."

I don't know if Merryshields is stronger than a witch. I wish I had some idea of how to measure them against each other - like, a witch could find gold but a house could turn gold to life, like it turned Silver to life. Does that make Merryshields stronger than Babs? You'd think so, seeing as it's such a massive house, but I've never met a witch before and I don't know anything about how powerful they might be. Especially Babs

Bembridge, Witch of the Seas, whose fearsome reputation must have some truth to it.

Mind you, I've never been in a house like this before, either.

I'm watching the door with all the strength of my eyes, and I'm certain I can see something move...

"Look," I whisper, but nobody hears me.

"Could we all jump on them and use their own ropes to tie them up?" Kit suggests.

"Brave lad," Two-Legs says, clapping him on the shoulder. "But I think we might find them too many to capture. We can fight them, though." He puts a hand on Taishi's shoulder. "I'll not let them take you, Taishi, boy. They'll take my life first."

"Babs's storm will stop us moving," Taishi says. "And if she pulls down the lightning..."

"Can she really...?" I hear Willow whisper, and Taishi nods unhappily.

"You guys--the door!" I say, flapping my hand to get their attention.

"No, we need to get them *through* this door; that'll be easier," Piper says. "Then at least they're confined... If we all work together..."

"But what if they split up, and she goes through the house?"

"*Guys*!" I stamp my foot. Finally, they stop rabbiting on.

"Wow," Taishi breathes. He has noticed what I've been trying to point out all along. "What is this place?"

The wooden door frame looks like it is turning back into a tree. Paint is flaking off and falling to the floor like glossy white snow, and small twigs are growing, stretching across the gap between the frame and the door.

"I told you," Kit says, with satisfaction.

"What kind of magic is this?" Johnny Two-Legs says wonderingly. His hat is clutched against his chest and a parrot perches on his shoulder. The others are sitting on the empty curtain rail, their heads moving as though they, too, are trying to understand.

There's a small commotion in the hall, as though two peo-ple are conferring in determined voices. The others, even Two-Legs, are stone-still. We listen hard while the house continues to grow quietly across the gaps. Tiny leaves sprout here and there as the branches get bigger, and on the end of one, a little apple blooms. Taishi is pointing at it wildly, while Kit grins beside him.

"Remember how I told you about Silver?" he mouths.

Silver, catching his name, thumps his tail on the floor and Piper hushes him. She makes more noise herself, to be honest. She looks strained.

The voices move closer. It sounds like there's an army of them, filling up the whole corridor. I'm glad that the Office Wing is so far away. There's no way the sound will travel that distance.

"What do you say, mistress?" one says. It's a man's voice, weedy and subservient. (Mam taught me that word, only she was describing something to do with women in the work-place. It was a bit of a rant to be honest, and I was mostly concentrating on Minecraft, but I got the general gist of what it meant.) Out of all the voices in the corridor, this one is definitely not the boss of the company.

"That's Danny," Two-Legs mutters. He's concentrating hard.

"Here," says someone else.

This voice isn't loud but it *is* strong - like when the strictest teacher at school speaks and the whole class falls quiet even though they weren't really talking in the first place. It was clearly used to being obeyed - or else. It makes me think of dark, unfriendly places, of being alone in the world, of being afraid. I don't want to hear her speak again.

Taishi mouths "Bembridge" at us and we all move closer together. Willow grips Piper's hand, her eyes shining with tears. Kit looks at me fearfully, both his arms wrapped around his dog. I lean forward and grab his shoulder to push him behind me, calculating the space between me and the door. If I grab one of the cushions, I think I could hit somebody pretty hard with it - when we have pillow fights, you definitely know about it if someone whacks you round the head. I feel a little bit better having some sort of a plan. The temperature in the room has dropped ten degrees. Two-Legs dips into a crouching position, like a tiger ready to pounce, his eyes not leaving the tree-door. I guess it's a bit like what Dad would look like if we were in danger. The thought of Dad makes me feel even sicker. My stomach feels like I went down in a lift and left it behind. I dart over and grab a cushion and then dash back again, holding it aloft in front of me and Kit.

"This door, mistress?" says a different woman.

"Neeves," Johnny whispers. "First mate."

"Yes," Babs Bembridge says. "It's small gold, and that means people, Neeves. Not enough to make up for the trouble I've gone to getting from that dratted island, but this house holds treasure, I can tell. Dispose of the adults and rope up the children. We'll leave them here. Collect them on the way back."

"Right you are, mistress," Neeves says. "Critchell, the rope."

There's the sound of a length of rope hitting the floor with a slap. "The monster'll wake soon enough," a man says.

"That's Critchell," Johnny murmurs.

Bembridge snorts. "That new mine on Jalletor Island needs some attention. They can go there. And if that swine John Two-Legs is with them, he can feed the monster - alone. Even missing an arm, he'll make a good snack." She laughs, a short sharp sound with no humour in it at all. "Hurry up untangling that rope, Critchell. I don't want to stand here all day watching you, you dog."

We don't dare to move, or even breathe. Footsteps approach the door, and I stare at the tree branches the house has grown. They look strong. Will they be strong enough? Kit's shaking behind me, peering from behind my back.

The door handle rattles.

"It's locked," Danny says.

"Don't be a fool," the witch replies. Her voice is horribly close. "This house is old. You should be able to break it. Get to it, crew."

"But mistress," someone says.

"That's Peg-Leg Pedro," Taishi mutters.

"You too, Pedro, you bonehead," Babs Bembridge snaps. "And Danny! Add your weight, you turkey."

A few seconds' silence, and then a rush of feet. A tremendous thud lands against the other side of the door. There are shouts of surprise from the hallway and, inside the room, we all flinch, Piper leaping backwards and dragging Willow with her.

"Ow!" Pedro's voice cries.

"Stop whining. Again," Babs Bembridge commands.

This time we are prepared for it, but it's no less frightening. The pirates yell as they charge at the door, and the crash when they collide with it is enormous. Cracks show in the bits of the door we can see, and paint flakes and apple blossoms scatter to the floor. Willow lets out a tiny whimper and one of the parrots squawks in fright.

"Mistress...my eye!" Critchell's voice wails.

Another man's voice chimes in. "The tree! There's a tree on the door! It spiked me!"

Johnny and Taishi look at each other. "Big Briggs?" Taishi says, and Johnny nods.

"For the sake of all that glitters!" Babs cries, somewhere between frustration and fury. "They are using magic! I won't have it! Here-"

There's a pause and a sound like distant, rumbling thunder. Johnny and Taishi draw closer together, their faces pale. I guess they have heard this sound before. But when nothing else happens, they look at each other in puzzlement.

Babs gives a cry of outrage.

What on earth is going on?

"No matter," the witch says, although her voice is humming with rage. "We'll leave them here." Her voice drops a little and we all lean forward to listen. "If they leave this room, I will track them, for as long as it takes, and they will regret the day they used magic against me. And you'll regret it too, Danny, if you let them get past you - you're staying here, to guard the door. The rest of you, come with me."

"Aye, mistress," Danny says, as the footsteps of Babs and the rest of her crewmates begin to move away.

Taishi is the first to speak. "We have to get out of this room before she comes back for us," he whispers urgently.

"There's nowhere safe to hide, lad," Johnny Two-Legs says gently, his voice a deep rumble. "No sense going back to the island - we can't overpower those left on the ship, nor can we sail it alone. Even so, I wouldn't leave these folk alone with that witch and her buccaneers loose in their house. Wouldn't be right." He takes a breath, looking around at us all. "And we can't run away. We've nowhere to go to. Babs would catch us, and all the worse for us if she did." He sighs, shaking his head. "No, Taishi lad. We must fight."

Us four cousins look at each other, feeling utterly hopeless.

"We don't know how many of them there are," Piper points out. "What if we go out there and she's brought the whole crew?"

Another thud against the door makes us jump again. "I know you're in there!" Danny shouts menacingly.

Two-Legs has been calculating something, his fingers stretched out and his mouth working silently. "She might have a few," he says, quickly and quietly, "but she won't have many. She'll have left a skeleton crew on board, so's nothing happens to the ship, and then there'll be a couple sailors left on the island, keeping guard there. She won't be expecting much resistance - she usually gets what she wants," he adds darkly. "Maybe her own swollen head will be her downfall. I heard Pedro out there, and that slimy cur Critchell, and first mate Neeves, the old cat-fish."

"And there was Big Briggs," Taishi adds. "A scabby bilge-rat, he is. I hate him. Once, he made me scrub the whole deck on my own, and then poured mouldy broth all over it so I had to do it again."

"We should just go straight out there and fight them!" Willow cries, and then says, "Ow!" as Piper elbows her sharply.

"Don't give our plan away! That Danny'll hear us through the door, you idiot!"

"No!" I cut in before Willow can argue back. I'd had a sudden flash of inspiration. "I've got it! We do nothing!"

Everyone stares at me as though I'm mad.

"I'm serious!" I say. "All we have to do is *follow* her!"

"What. Are. You. Talking. About?" Piper asks me through gritted teeth.

"Listen," I hiss, speaking as quickly and as quietly as I can. "If she can use her magic to find gold, and we know the house has treasure somewhere, why don't we let her find it for us?"

They are still staring at me, so I give them a second to catch up. My heart thumps. My ears strain to hear the direction the footsteps of Babs and her crew are taking through the house.

"He's got it!" Johnny Two-Legs breathes, slapping me so hard on the shoulder that I stumble. "Good lad, Jack. We'll follow her - she'll be that distracted by the gold in front of her, she won't think to look behind her. Taishi and I will help ya - it's the least we can do after you saved us from that island. After all, if it hadn't been for you, we'd likely be back on that ship - or looking at the inside of her monster, more like," he adds, shuddering.

Kit is straining to hear through the apple leaves at the door. "What is that weird noise?"

We listen. The clatter of the retreating crew has faded, but there is still an odd, small banging sound.

"Peg-Leg Pedro," Johnny whispers, so quietly we can barely hear him. "He's slow - he'll be following her. He's afraid of Bembridge, too, but fear makes him a coward. You just have to be careful to avoid Pedro's leg."

"What?" I ask, confused. "His <u>leg</u>? Why?"

"He built a gun within it," Taishi explains. "He can't move fast, but he's an excellent shot. He can down a bird from half a mile."

"Oh," I say weakly.

"What will we do when Bembridge has the treasure?" Piper asks quietly.

I flap my hand at her to shut her up. Pedro's footsteps are getting fainter. "We'll figure that out later," I breathe.

Danny's steps continue back and forth outside the door, slow and steady. Sweat prickles up my back. I put my hand on Kit's shoulder again, but don't dare to move him.

Two-Legs whispers urgently at us. "I'm going to rush him and knock him out," he says, cracking his knuckles meaning-fully. "You're going to follow Bembridge. I'll make my way back to the window on the island, and close it, then stop any of the others coming through until you get back." He pulls a length of twine out from his pocket. "Must be a way to tie that window so's it won't come loose again."

I can't hear the crew's footsteps at all now; even Pedro's are very faint. I'm terrified we'll have lost them somewhere in the house. I nod frantically at Two-Legs. "Yes! Good plan, let's do it!"

Before I've even taken a breath, Two-Legs reaches between the branches and puts his hand on the door handle. As if the house has been listening to us, the apple tree branches move out of the way as easily as if they are made of silk. Johnny Two-Legs yanks open the door and barges out with a low, furious roar, knocking the bonehead Danny off his feet. Danny is sweaty and red, with a belly that hangs over his trousers and grubby flip-flops on his dirty feet. He pushes himself up to standing with difficulty and balls his fists ready to punch, but Two-Legs is too quick for him. Even though Two-Legs has only one arm, I can see that he is the better fighter by far.

I'm desperate to stay and watch, but equally desperate not to lose what might be our only chance at finding the treasure.

"Come on!" Willow hisses at me. "We've got to run - but *quietly*!"

We scamper along the corridor, following Kit, who has rushed ahead. I can't resist turning at the sound of a body hitting the floor with a solid-sounding <u>thump.</u> To my relief, I see Danny lying still on the floor. Johnny Two-Legs stands over him, punching the air in victory. He sees me looking and gives a thumbs-up and a big grin that I can see through his beard.

Kit, Willow, Piper and Taishi pause before a corner, next to a circular window. The wooden frame has grown a cluster of small branches over Willow's head, and flowers are blossoming right next to her hair. They are all staring at it, amazed.

"Look!" Piper says to me, pointing at the unfurling leaves.

"Incredible," I say, and it is, but time is ticking on fast. "Kit, what's going on?"

Kit peers round the corner and quickly whips his head back around to face us. "They're walking straight on," he reports, his voice scratchy with silence. "Babs has got her fingers stretched out in front of her, and Pedro is a bit behind."

Willow strokes a blossom petal that drifts past her cheek. "Don't worry, house," she whispers. "We'll do our best to get them out of here."

I half-register Willow's conversation with the house, but mainly I'm still thinking of a plan. That's what a captain must do at all times, after all, even when the sweat is sliding down his back and his knees are shaking. A captain needs to lead the way... and have a few back-up plans just in case things go wrong.

"Right," I mutter to the others. "We follow at a distance, without attracting their attention, and wait for Babs to find the treasure. Then we take them out."

"What do you mean?" Piper asks. She's clasped her hands together and is squeezing her fingers.

"Shouldn't be too hard to knock Peg-Leg Pedro to the floor," I say. "Willow and Kit, you can do that. He might be an adult, but we'll have the element of surprise."

"Right," Willow says, and Kit nods, his eyes wide but his mouth firm.

"I can get his leg so he can't start shooting," Taishi offers with resolve. "I saw him take it off to clean it once - I'm pretty sure I can twist it off if you two sit on him so he can't move?"

There is the faintest hint of excitement on Kit's face now a plan is starting to form. "What about the others?" he asks.

"We'll fight them all... somehow," Willow says. She looks around the empty corridor, as though searching for a weapon. An apple falls from the branch, making us all jump, and Taishi picks it up.

"This'll keep us going," he says, and starts to take a huge bite - but as his teeth fasten around it, he yelps. "It's solid!" he says in surprise. "Why is it solid?"

Willow reaches up to feel the branch it came from, but to our astonishment, the whole thing breaks off in her hand. "What?" she asks in alarm.

"Look!" I say, pointing. "Look how you're holding it! It's like a <u>sword</u>, Willow! It's a weapon! Merryshields is giving us something to fight the others with!"

"A solid apple?" Taishi says, unconvinced, as he stares at the fruit in his hand.

"Chuck it at someone's head," I advise.

Taishi looks at Piper.

"Not me!" she squeals, putting her hands up.

"Catch," he says, with a small laugh, and throws it at her.

Amazingly, she catches it. "It's pretty weighty," she says, dropping it from hand to hand. "You could do some damage with this. Is that why you're still holding a pillow?" she asks me with a cheeky grin.

I drop the cushion, which I'd kept hold of automatically. "Actually, yes. Remember the last time we had a pillow fight, how much you complained when I walloped you round the head?"

"Fine," she says, obviously not wanting to remember her massive defeat.

"But I think it'll just slow me down," I tell her now. "I can run faster without carrying anything, because my plan -- Willow! You nearly took my eye out!"

Willow is waving her stick sword around. "This makes me feel a lot better," she admits. "Hey, Taishi, try touching that branch." She points.

He does, and to his amazement, the branch thickens beneath his palm, and then drops off, right at his feet. He picks it up and tosses it in his hands to get a feel for the weight. "Thank you...?" he says shyly to the walls, not quite sure where to look.

Willow grins, though her smile doesn't cover her whole face. "You're obviously one of us!" she says.

"Great," I say, trying to continue with the plan even though they are all getting distracted, what with Willow and Taishi spinning their sticks and Piper chucking her apple up and down. "I'll snatch whatever it is that Bembridge finds. And then," I continue, watching the plan unfurl in my mind, "I'll take the treasure and sprint - don't look like that, Pi, you know I'm a faster runner than you - back to the Island. They should all follow me then, so you all follow on after them as fast as you can. Fight them off enough to hold them back, but then run away as soon as they follow me. Get back to the apple tree room, where we were just now. The house will keep you safe again, I think," I am speaking even more quickly now, for fear that the pirates will go out of sight and make all my planning useless. Another apple drops to the floor and I take that as a yes.

"I'll race across the island and lure the pirates away, then race back to the door," I say, picking up the apple for Kit. "Two-Legs will have closed the window by that point, so the door will be the only way on or off that island. If I get out before they realise I've circled them, they'll be stuck there with no way back." My heart is racing in anticipation.

"It's a good plan," Willow says, tapping me encouragingly with her stick.

I grin at her. It is a sound plan; I have to admit.

"Assuming Babs Bembridge even finds anything," Piper murmurs, tugging one of her plaits. I nudge her with my elbow.

"Think positive, Pi," I tell her. "Don't forget, we've got Merryshields on our side."

Kit is still on lookout. "They're almost at the end of the next corridor," he whispers. "Bembridge is pointing at a door straight ahead...is that more stairs, do you think?"

"Must be," Willow shrugs.

"Kit, scout ahead," I say. "We need to know which floor they come out on."

Kit nods and scampers off, practically silent on the dusty floor.

"Come on," I say to the others, and we hurry after him.

He's hovering halfway down the stairs when we get there. "Just one floor," he mouths. "I'll go ahead."

I nod and we follow. At the next floor down, Kit is again peering through the door along the landing.

"We haven't explored here at all." Piper sounds nervous.

"She's found a room..." Kit whispers. He's staring intently through the tiny gap. "She's trying to open the door, but she can't... Peg-Leg Pedro's caught up with them, just about."

Willow gasps. "What if *that's* the room that needs the key?" she exclaims.

"What key?" Piper asks, frowning.

"The key from Headquarters, remember!" Willow hisses.

With a rush, I remember coming into Headquarters and seeing Willow holding up a strange little key in her hand. All the nervousness and excitement we felt when we were just beginning to uncover the mysteries of Merryshields sweeps over me again. I let out a low, soft whistle. "Feels like ages since we found that in Headquarters," I say.

"Pedro's throwing himself against the door, but nothing's happening," Kit interrupts, pulling us all back into the moment.

"He's not having a good day with doors," I smirk.

"Now the others are all trying it, like they did upstairs," Kit says. "Bembridge looks angry... She's trying the handle again - it's opened!" He glances at me over his shoulder. "Maybe it was just a door like our old living room one, where you had to wiggle it a certain way."

"Maybe the house has let them in for a reason," I suggest.

Kit turns back. "Well, whatever it is, they look really surprised. Ok, they're all going in..."

"Are they out of sight?" I ask.

Kit nods.

"Ok then," I say, and take a breath. "Are you ready, girls? Taishi? As soon as they've found the treasure, we fight. I take the gold and they chase after me. You chase after them. Got it?"

They nod, faces drawn with worry.

"Come on, then," I say, squishing my fear down and pulling up my courage. "Let's go."

In The Jungle

Piper

W e creep along the corridor behind Kit. When he stops at a door with mangos carved all over it, we shuffle along the wall and carefully peer round the doorframe into the room. What we see takes my breath away.

The room is just like one of those you see in historic mansions or in an old-fashioned drama on TV. There is panelling around the walls and in each panel is the most gorgeous, sumptuous wallpaper in a leafy pattern--all in different shades of greens and blues, but with the occasional pink flower shooting up. The edge of each panel is carved and edged with gold. There is a four-poster bed with dusty green curtains tied back against the posts and a deep wooden chest at the foot of it. At the far end of the room, there is an enormous stone fireplace with a small, hard-backed chair before it. Dotted along the walls are several low bookcases, each with a variety of leather-bound books, odd little ornaments and shallow drawers. Apart from the gold on the wall, I can't see anything that might have drawn Babs Bembridge and her witchy fingers here.

Two of the pirates are eagerly rifling through the wooden chest. One of them lifts up a dress and holds it against herself, looking down admiringly.

"Neeves and Critchell," Taishi mutters in my ear. "First mate," he adds, and I see that the woman, Neeves, is wearing a jacket that's a scruffy version of Babs Bembridge's.

"I've seen them before!" Willow squeaks, poking me in the back. Her eyes are fearful and I remember how scared she was that night she went back onto the island. I squeeze her hand.

"Ugh, look at the witch," Jack murmurs, his shoulders wriggling as he watches.

He's right, it's weird. Babs Bembridge is standing in the middle of the room with her hands stretched out in front of her, moving wildly from side to side. Her brown hair is pulled back into a low, loose ponytail, and she is wearing a long brown jacket trimmed in silver thread that flares out at the hem. She has a silver ring on each of her thumbs which glint as she moves - and she is moving like *crazy*! She's quivering and shaking, from her fingers up through her whole body, and her face is creepily blank as though she isn't really looking at the room, but trying to see what her fingers are telling her.

I glance at Taishi. He looks as frightened as he did up in the apple tree room, and my whole stomach starts to twist. There are two other pirates in the room, as well as Neeves and Critchell. Peg-Leg Pedro - obvious because of the shiny black wooden leg that sticks out from his dirty trousers - and a big, strong-looking man who must be Big Briggs. How on earth are we supposed to defeat all these - what had Johnny Two-Legs called them? Buccaneers? I swallow and grip Willow's hand tighter.

As we watch, one of Babs's hands picks a clear direction and her arm flies around to point at one of the bookcases. Her other hand swings madly towards a blank bit of wall.

"She's got a glitch," Jack mutters. "There's clearly nothing there."

The witch takes a huge, shuddering breath. "Look in those shelves," she commands, and Neeves drops the dress and darts to the shelves.

I feel a nudge against my leg and look down to see Silver, who has been sniffing the air urgently. I think he's desperate to get up close to the pirates and inhale their fishy, greasy smell. Dogs are weird like that. The grosser something smells, the more they want to investigate it. Kit has his fingers in Silver's collar, so as the dog lurches forward, Kit is taken along with him. I reach out to stop them and hold Kit back, but Silver's tail slips right through my fingers.

Jack, Willow, Taishi and I watch in horror as Kit is pulled into the room, unable to do anything. My heart is in my mouth and I whip my head around the door to watch Kit, counting on the others to keep an eye out and pull me back if it looks like one of the pirates is going to see me. Critchell has kicked the chair upside down, Pedro is looking up the fireplace and Babs is fixated on the empty wall; luckily, they don't seem to hear Silver's clickety-clacking claws on the floor or notice Kit as he ducks down beside the bed. He's on his knees with both arms around Silver, holding him back from the pirates.

Then Babs flings an arm out in Kit's direction.

Kit automatically leaps backwards... and *disappears from view*!

Willow pulls her hand out of mine because I squeeze it so hard. I risk peeking my head even further into the room, feeling as though it's going to get blown off any second, and stare at the spot Kit was crouching in just seconds before. My heart nearly stops. (I can't count how many times that has happened since we've been in this house.) There is Kit, waving cheerfully at me from *inside the wallpaper*!

I shove Jack and grin, pointing silently around the door at his younger brother. Relief washes over Jack's face. He glances at Babs and her cronies, and then steps neatly into the wallpaper beside Kit, immediately becoming part of the blue-green pattern. They high-five one another soundlessly and move up to make space for us. I can see Kit saying something, his face moving excitedly, but I can't hear a word coming out of his mouth.

"In the wallpaper," I hiss at Willow and Taishi, and I step in after Jack before they can ask any questions, hoping they will figure it out.

The first thing I notice inside the wallpaper is the smell, and the second is the noise. It's warm and damp and humid, with a pungent, slightly tangy aroma like a million things are growing all around me. Mangoes hang ripe and round everywhere I look. Noise fills up all the available space. There is every kind of bird song, frogs croaking, insects chirruping and the sound of water dripping and running everywhere. Something calls out on one side of us and an answering call comes from behind.

My hair sticks to my cheeks and I jump as my fingers brush against the hairy leaf of a deep blue plant. The colour in here is so weird! It is exactly the same as the wallpaper--all different shades of blues and greens, definitely not what you would find in an actual jungle. Pea green tree trunks, sapphire leaves, teal-blue stems, bright blue mangos (Mum got us one once--they are not blue!). There's the odd bright pink flower, which looks strange against the turquoise fronds and emerald stalks. High, high above us, the leaves move in an invisible breeze. I'm still holding the apple the house gave us in the corridor and notice it has stayed the same colour, just like we have; so now, it's us who look odd in amongst all the green-blue foliage.

Willow slides in beside me, followed by Taishi who stares around with wide eyes.

"What *is* this place?!" he says, not for the first time today.

"Isn't our house the best?" Willow laughs delightedly.

"Shh!" I say automatically, but Jack nudges me, grinning.

"They can't hear us!" he says. "We couldn't hear the jungle from the other side of the wallpaper, so when we're in here, nobody can hear us out there!"

"It's incredible," Willow says, touching the thick bark of a tall sea-green tree.

The boys hoot with laughter.

"This is *amazing*!" Taishi says, pointing at the pirates with his branch. "Look at them! They don't have a clue we're here!"

I've been so busy looking around that I'd temporarily for-gotten about the room in front of me. "This is so weird," I say slowly.

It's like looking through a window without the glass. A sort of thin, shimmery membrane separates us from the room in the real world. Peg-Leg Pedro has stopped sticking his head up the chimney and is crouched awkwardly on the other side of the bed, looking under the bedside table. He looks as clear as he was when we were in the doorway, but we can't hear him and he quite obviously can't hear us, either. Briggs, Critchell and Neeves are desperately pulling every book and ornament from every shelf, in hopes of satisfying the visibly angry witch.

Taishi's grip tightens around the branch the house gave him. "Look at her," he says, his eyes fixed on Babs Bembridge. "She's sensing loads of stuff." He looks terrified.

Looking at Babs, I don't blame him. She's still shaking all over and her hands are going nuts, leaping towards one point and then another, like she's about to explode with the pressure. The other pirates glance at her as they work with a mixture of fear and awe. Babs makes an impatient jerking gesture and walks so close to the empty wall that her nose is almost touching it. I'm sure she can't see the real-life jungle behind the wallpaper. She'd be looking a lot more astounded. I dare to feel a bit hopeful - it feels as though the house is truly on our side, with magic we could never have imagined.

Babs Bembridge runs her hands all over the wallpaper, leaving greasy marks where her fingers skim the surface.

"Dad would go bananas if he saw that," Kit points out.

"What is she doing?" Jack asks.

"Touching the walls!" Kit says. "You know Dad and walls!"

"I mean, what is she doing *to* the walls?" Jack rolls his eyes.

"Her fingers guided her to that spot," I say. "One hand point-ed at the bookshelves, and the other pointed towards the wall."

"Do you think there's gold, like, *behind* the wallpaper?" Jack asks, interested.

"Or somewhere in this jungle, maybe?" Willow suggests. "I mean, she might be able to sense it, even in here."

"She can't get in, though," Kit says with interest, watching as Babs bangs the wall in frustration. "Maybe only people who live here can do the house magic." He notices Taishi and corrects himself. "Or maybe only *children*...?"

"Or maybe," Taishi says, with surprising insight, "maybe the house only lets certain people have access to its magic. It protected Two-Legs as well," he reminds us, "when it grew that apple tree to keep us safe upstairs. And it gave me my branch, and it opened the door to this room. So maybe it decides who goes where."

"That's a good point," Willow says, leaning so close to the shimmery wall that I have to pull her backwards in case she falls through it back into the room again.

"But why there...?" I wonder out loud. "Why would she be drawn to that *particular* bit of wall? Unless..." A thought strikes me - what if there's a secret corridor, and Babs can sense it?! There's no way of telling without going around, and I don't dare to move just yet.

"I hope the pirates don't think Silver is a treasure," Kit says suddenly.

"Surely not," Willow says. "He's a real dog, he's not worth anything - except to us, of course," she adds hurriedly.

"Yeah," Kit says, as everyone looks at him. "Anyone can see that he's not actually made of silver any more... "

All of us gasp and freeze, except Kit. Even though it goes against every instinct I have, I move slowly towards him, my hand extended. "Don't move," I say, keeping my voice as steady as possible.

"Uh...why?" Kit asks nervously, following my instruction. "What are you doing, Piper?"

"Rescuing you from a giant spider!" I exclaim, grabbing the biggest leaf I can and using it to divert a lime green tarantula that was creeping towards Kit's head. Kit shrieks and leaps out of the way.

"Quick thinking, Piper," Jack says.

I smile. "Thanks."

There's a brief silence as Kit shuffles closer to Jack, shuddering. "Hey," he says, looking back into the room. "What's Babs doing now?"

Taishi shakes his head. "I've never seen her like this before," he says.

The witch's mouth opens terribly in a shout (that we can't hear) and flings herself back towards another one of the bookcases. She screams and Briggs and Pedro drop what they're holding and leap towards it.

"What on earth is in there?" Willow asks, her voice tight with fear. My chest is full of nerves. I feel like my heart is twitching as badly as Babs's fingers.

"It's just books," Kit says, as the pirates begin flinging the books out one by one, dodging out of the way of the witch's flying hands. When the case is empty, they rip out the two little drawers. Then they pick it up and start to shake it, Babs Bembridge shivering over them in fury.

"There's something there," Taishi says.

Jack nods. "I bet she's using all the words our mam uses when she thinks we're not listening."

We laugh weakly. It helps a little, but my stomach is still churning.

Willow is swinging her arms around and stretching like they make us do in PE. Taishi raises his eyebrows at her in confusion.

"Are you getting warmed up, Will?" Jack smirks.

"You might laugh," Willow says seriously, "but if we're going to stop five fully grown people, including a <u>witch</u>, from escaping, I want to be completely ready." She starts running on the spot, lunging every now and then from side to side. "I wish they'd hurry up," she says. "The waiting is driving me mad."

Taishi nods. "Me too," he says, and starts copying Willow, jogging on the spot with his arms out and making his knees hit his apple tree branch. He looks from the branch to the jungle around us. "Do you think your house will help us again?" he asks.

I shrug. "I don't know," I say, wishing I did. I believe that Merryshields doesn't want anything bad to happen to us, but I don't know how much it's capable of.

"Hang on," Jack says, nudging Taishi into me accidentally so that we both stumble and land on the thick leaf carpet. "Do you think they're going to take the whole bookcase with them?!"

"Will that make things easier or harder?" Willow muses, lifting her branch up and down above her head.

Jack screws up his nose. We call it his thinking face when he does that. It's just like Uncle Peter's, only without the glasses. "Well, it'll be easier to knock them down if they're holding it," he says at last. "But harder for me to pick it up and run with it. If-"

"They aren't taking it anywhere," Willow interrupts, as the pirates stop shaking the case and set it on its side.

"They're trying to get into it from the back," Jack says, looking relieved. He narrows his eyes and peers closer with interest. "There must be a secret compartment or something."

As we watch, Pedro pulls a tool out of his pocket and slides it roughly into a gap in the wood.

"He's going to damage it!" Willow cries. "Ooo, Mum's going to be mad."

"As long as we don't get the blame, I don't care," Jack says darkly.

"He's in! He's opened it!" Kit says. Peg-Leg Pedro has wrenched off the back of the case. Broken shards of wood litter the floor around them.

Babs Bembridge is smiling. It is really creepy. She pushes Peg-Leg out of the way and reaches into the yawning black space behind the drawer. We all gasp as a look of triumph lights up her face, and she pulls out something absolutely incredible.

Battle For Treasure

Kit

"What *is* that?" I ask, straining to see as Silver bounces up and down next to me, my hand through his collar.

Bad Babs is holding something that's gleaming gold in the light from the window. I can feel myself light up! This is incredible! Merryshields *does* have treasure!

"They're... jaguars? Yes, jaguars!" Willow cries. "They're incredible!"

"There are *two*?" I shout, and then as the witch turns to show them off to the other pirates, I see that there *are* two. She holds one of the golden ornaments in each hand; one of them lying down and one frozen mid-pounce.

"They're huge," Jack says, his eyes shining.

"They're *valuable*," Taishi adds.

I ignore Silver, who is now whimpering at me in his desperation to be free, and peer at the newly discovered treasure. Bad Babs holds one up to the light streaming in from the window and I can see that it is the most incredible ornament I've ever seen. Even more amazing than Silver was (before he was a real dog, I mean), and that's saying something. (Although, I obviously wouldn't want a jaguar for a pet.) The gold is soft and shiny and it seems to glow from the inside. It has bright green jewels for eyes that sparkle as Bad Babs moves it through the air.

"Those must be emeralds!" Jack says. He sounds amazed. "Gold and emeralds! That's *proper* treasure!"

"Well, we've got to get it from her then," Willow says, sounding nervous again.

"I know," Jack says, his voice determined. "Are we all ready? We're all going to rush out of there together. I'm going to snatch those jaguars right out of her horrible witchy hands, and then run back to the island. Hopefully, she'll follow me. And you four are going to distract the others and stop Peg-Leg Pedro from shooting me. Alright?"

He almost makes it sound easy. Willow and Taishi look at each other, nodding and swinging their branches up and down. Piper nods and grips her apple. I feel butterflies suddenly rushing up under my ribs. "What about Silver?" I ask.

"Let him loose to run around barking. He'll add to the general chaos," Jack instructs.

As though he's listening to us, Silver woofs, and narrows his eyes at the witch and pirates. Well, I *think* it's them he's looking at, at first. But with a rush, I see one of the jaguars blink... with a rush, I realise the pirates aren't what's caused Silver's attention at all.

I don't have time to tell Jack. Before I can say a word, Silver charges through the cling-film stuff that separates us from the room, making one of the loudest, fiercest barks I have ever heard.

"WOOF WOOF WOOF!"

We definitely succeed in startling the pirates. I almost forget what my mission is, I'm so distracted by the thought that those jaguars might come to life, but as Willow races past me, I am pulled back into the action and burst into the room alongside Jack, Piper and Taishi.

"RAAAAAAAA!!" I roar, adding to the noise Silver is making as he barks his head off some more. He jumps at Peg-Leg Pedro in a streak of silver.

"Damn ye, ye little scullion!" Pedro cries, toppling to the floor. I hear the singing sound of metal and realise that Critchell, Neeves and Briggs have drawn their big, curved swords.

"Jack! Look out!" I shout, as Big Briggs charges towards him. Jack jumps up onto the bed out of the way, his eyes on Bad Babs. Babs is clutching her treasure to her chest and she looks furious.

"Get them, you sodden-witted toads!" she yells.

Pedro has shoved Silver off him, so Willow and I jump onto the stinky pirate instead, each of us pinning one arm to the ground. Taishi jumps over and twists at Peg-Leg Pedro's wooden peg leg. In seconds it comes off with a POP! that I can hear over the sound of swords swishing through the air. As I look around me, not quite sure where to go or what to do first, I notice that it's not just swords that are swishing. Willow grips her branch tightly in both hands, swinging it fiercely to give Taishi time to jump away from Pedro as the pirate grabs at him. Piper is jumping from foot to foot, tossing her apple from one hand to the other as Critchell laughs nastily, approaching her as though he's not worried about a kid at all.

Meanwhile, Jack is using the post at the end of the bed to balance as he kicks out towards Briggs. The big man stumbles backwards, loses his footing and slips, dropping his cutlass. The room is small for this many people to be charging around, but maybe that's a good thing--there's less room for their swords.

Neeves is staying out of the action for now, guarding Babs with her cutlass drawn and her face wicked.

"Dare to come at me, you measly scut!" she shouts at Jack, who is leaping from side to side, trying to draw her out.

Willow and I leap off Peg-Leg Pedro.

"Kit, be lookout!" she yells, and I immediately dart towards one of the bookshelves, thinking I can climb onto it to see what's going on. But I trip backwards and Critchell grabs my arms! I shout in alarm. He pulls them behind my back, gripping his cutlass between his teeth, and begins to drag me towards the witch. I struggle with all my might, but he is so strong. He stinks of oil and fish. I kick out desperately. Then Silver, still barking, leaps towards the scruffy, oily pirate and bites him hard on the arm. Critchell lets go of me, howling in pain, and sinks to the floor. His cutlass has fallen down and I kick it away from him without his noticing. Silver rushes to my side and I bury my face in his fur.

"Thanks buddy," I whisper.

Piper catches my eye to make sure I'm OK – I nod, and she rushes forward to help Jack. I climb up onto the bookshelf to watch the action, my eyes running all over the room at my brother, cousins and friend, all fighting the horrible pirates.

"Go on, Piper!" I shout. Piper dances around in front of Babs and Neeves, calling them both names. Her face looks defiant, but I can tell she's as scared as I am.

"You stinking old witch!" she yells. "You slimy rotten cabbage face!"

I see Jack flash a quick look at her and I think if he wasn't concentrating so hard, he might have grinned. "Watch out!" I yell. Jack darts this way and that, narrowly missing Neeves's cutlass as she slices it through the air.

My heart is hammering so hard I think it might burst.

But then I jump as I hear Willow snarl in a very un-Willow way. She is waving her stick at Briggs, jabbing and poking the branch at him - and it's working. Briggs is stuck in the narrow space between the bed and the wall, one arm covering his face as she jabs at him, the other hand grappling for his cutlass.

"Amazing, Willow, you've got him!" I cheer. But I can't celebrate - Taishi is in the thick of it with Critchell and my heart is in my mouth.

Critchell, still nursing his dog-bite wound, tries to get up from the floor, but Taishi swings at him with his apple tree branch, too. But before he can land the blow, Critchell snatches the other end of the branch and the pair begin a sort of angry tug-of-war over it, Critchell swearing at Taishi and Taishi's face angry and afraid at the same time. I don't know how to help. I'm just preparing to leap off the bookshelf when Taishi suddenly lets go of the branch and Critchell collapses back onto the floor. Taishi leaps into the nearest panel of wallpaper and vanishes into the jungle. I watch him disappear amongst the leaves, looking all blue, and wonder what on earth he is doing. This wasn't part of the plan.

I don't have time to wonder for long, though. Critchell pushes himself up again and thrusts the newly won branch sword defensively at Silver, who is growling at him, his lips pulled right back over his teeth. He looks fierce, like a shimmery wolf.

"Avast ye!" Babs yells at her buccaneers, her voice hoarse with frenzy. "Give no quarter! Scupper them, you lily-livered dogs!"

She lunges at Piper from beneath Neeves's arm, and Piper squeaks and jumps away, vanishing into the wallpaper in another panel on the wall just like Taishi. Babs and Neeves are both distracted by this, gasping as Piper disappears. Jack takes the opportunity to duck past Neeves and barrel into Babs, knocking her sideways. But Briggs has got away from Willow and leapt across the bed! Willow is looking a bit stunned on the floor, her branch just out of reach, and I see the whites all around her eyes as she watches Briggs throw his beefy arms around Jack, sending both of them crashing to the floor.

A ball of anger bursts out of me. "Get off my brother!" I yell, and I jump down towards him - but then I freeze.

Pedro has squirmed around on the floor. He's reached his peg leg, and he's pulled out his gun.

He cocks it with an evil grin, and then a massive, explosive noise reverberates all round the room.

The Golden Jaguars

Willow

There is a stunned silence, and then Bad Babs lets out a shout of laughter that goes right through my tummy. I wriggle off the floor and up onto the bed, away from her.

"Ha! Now you're for it, you filthy little scoundrels!" She cackles delightedly at Pedro, but then looks scathingly around at her crew. Neeves is still dancing around in front of her, Briggs has Jack pinned to the floor and Critchell is poking at Silver with the stick, a stupid grin on his big ugly face. "It seems I brought the weakest members of my crew... mark my words: I won't be making that mistake again." Upon hearing Babs' words, all three of the pirates freeze and I see fear in their eyes.

"At least *one* of you half-witted sea-worms," Babs continues in her ice-hard voice, "has found some guts!" She winks at Pedro, who has pulled himself up to stand on one leg, balancing against the wall (which, of course, *he* doesn't fall through), his gun aimed straight at Jack.

I feel sick with dread. No matter how quick or clever we are, there's nothing we can do about a gun. Everything turned around so quickly; just a moment ago, I could have sworn they were losing. Kit looks close to tears, stuck in a corner of the room amongst all the books and bits that the pirates had thrown on the floor, but I can't see Taishi anywhere - did he escape while I wasn't looking? At least Piper is safe. I saw her vanish into the jungle. Surely she'll think of something to help us - I just hope it's in time.

"Get your ropes," Bad Babs commands. "Tie the puny minnows up."

"Ready for the mines?" Neeves gloats at me, her hands undoing the ropes that are fastened around her waist as she takes threatening steps towards me.

"The mines are too good for 'em," Critchell growls, holding his injured arm. "Them and this dog can go *straight* to the monster."

Kit lets out a whimper that makes all the pirates laugh out loud. *Piper, where are you?* I think urgently. Then, behind the dirty grinning face of Pedro, I see something flying through the air *in the jungle*.

"Piper's apple!" I shout.

The pirates laugh even harder, thinking I'm spouting nonsense, but the others look at me with a tiny twinkling of hope.

"But..." Jack calls back to me as he struggles madly against Briggs, "did *Piper* throw it?"

I immediately see his point. Piper is the worst thrower of all of us. I squint into the wallpaper, backing away from the advancing Neeves. Behind the spinning apple I see Piper running at full speed towards us.

"Yes," I cry, my heart sinking again. At the very least, it'll cause a distraction. I grab tighter hold of my stick as Critchell lurches for Silver with an outstretched length of rope. But as Piper's apple pops through the thin membrane of the wallpaper, it *changes course* all on its own! Instead of heading straight over Pedro's shoulder, it is now travelling at full speed straight towards his head.

THUNK!

The one-legged pirate topples to the floor, knocked out cold.

Jack cheers in a muffled sort of way from under Brigg's arm and Kit shouts, "Ha! Didn't see *that* coming, did you?!" Neeves's hands drop away from the ropes at her waist, and she stops at the end of the bed, not knowing whether to look at me or at Babs Bembridge.

Babs lets out a howl of rage and puts her arms out to either side of her. She is clearly beginning to summon magic in a witchy sort of way. "I'll get control of you, you little scumbags," she says, the jaguars quivering in her hands. The room seems to pulse with energy. I start to feel wobbly and put my hands on the wall to steady myself, forgetting for a moment that I can't lean against it.

"Help us, house!" I plead, as my fingers slip into the jungly blue. Babs is humming and I see to my astonishment that the ceiling is no longer covered in cracked white paint, but has morphed into thick, dark clouds that are swirling faster and faster above us. Fat drops of rain fly through the air and the witch smiles horribly.

"Now you've got it coming to you, you little brats!" Critchell sneers, stabbing his cutlass towards Kit and Silver who are hovering in the corner of the room, unable to escape. "I'll spike you with the point of my sword, and she can fry you with a sharp bolt of lightning."

Piper erupts out of the wallpaper. "Hey!" she roars. "Pick on someone your own size!" She dips to the floor mid-run, scooping up her apple from the floor beside Pedro's motion-less body and throws it as hard as she can towards Critchell. I feel a swell of pride and almost want to cheer out loud. *That's my sister!!*

The apple soars through the air and Kit picks up a book to protect his head, having been on the receiving end of Piper's throws before. But once again, the house corrects the course of the apple. It slams into Critchell's wounded arm and he pivots and stumbles, landing on the floor with a splash. Kit throws the book at him for good measure, hitting him in the face.

"Ha," Piper says with satisfaction.

Kit laughs weakly and jumps over Critchell to bound onto the bed beside me. I grip him with one hand, blinking rain-drops out of my eyes and grasping my apple tree branch, ready to fend off more attacks.

"Where's Silver?" Kit pants.

Piper squeezes my shoulder. "Just got to help Taishi," she says breathlessly, and pops back into the jungle again.

Briggs gives a sudden high-pitched squeal and jerks away from Jack, who wriggles free and leaps up onto the bed beside us. Silver pops up from beside him, grinning with all of his teeth on show. The dog shakes the water from his fur, although it's pointless - the rain is falling thick and fast.

"Good boy, Silver!" Jack pants, patting him as Kit drags him closer. "Is it me, or is it like forty degrees in here?"

I don't know what the temperature is, but I do know that it's hot - and humid. I've never been in a sauna, but Mum told me once that they're very hot and very damp, and that's exactly what this is like. Babs is standing beneath the centre of the storm, her eyes closed. Neeves has completely unwrapped her ropes now, and is advancing around the bed towards us, cackling nastily.

"I'll wait til you're fried, then I'll tether you," she cries. "Not long now and she'll be bringing down the lightning!"

Jack, Kit and I huddle together, watching helplessly as the clouds swirl and spin furiously around the humming witch. I can't help but check the jungle again and again, hoping to see Piper or Taishi. Briggs has joined Neeves, one hand clutching his backside where Silver must have bitten him. The pair of them form a sort of barrier in front of Babs. There's no way we can get to the jaguars without one of those wickedly sharp cutlasses cutting us down. Critchell is making his way over to them, staggering awkwardly for some reason that I can't understand.

"Did you bite him too?" I ask Silver.

"He did - on the arm," Kit says. "Look, Willow!"

I look. Through the wallpaper, I see Piper and Taishi returning from the depths of the jungle, both with their hands full of something that looks like piles of wriggling snakes.

"What are they doing?" Jack asks.

"Look at the floor!" Kit cries, and suddenly I see why Critchell is moving so strangely.

Creeping vines have covered the floor, spreading from the bottoms of the walls and all over the carpet. They are moving and growing and sliding over each other, bright blues and greens, so thick that soon we cannot see the floor at all. One of Critchell's feet has been caught in a loop and he can't pull it free, no matter how hard he yanks. He tries to use Neeves as leverage but she shakes him off, not noticing the vines inching closer to her boots.

"Get off, you fool," she snarls. "We'll need both hands in a minute to tie these measly rampallions up. Soon as Captain zaps them..."

But Babs has opened her eyes, and the look on her face is murderous.

"She can't do it," Kit says gleefully, kneeling up. "Merryshields' magic is too strong for her! She can't make the lightning!"

"I'll show you, you flap-mouthed barnacle!" Babs screams at him, shaking both hands towards Kit, but I think he is right.

"Here!" Taishi yells, popping through the wallpaper into the pouring rain. It must be raining in the jungle, too. His hair is plastered to his face and so is Piper's, who plops out beside him, gasping for breath. They stumble on the moving vines but don't fall. Their arms are filled with thick, ropy vines, and no sooner are they out of the jungle then the vines seem to slide out of their arms of their own accord, and begin to wend their slippery way across the wet floor towards the pirates.

"What...?!" Neeves shrieks, finally noticing the magic advancing towards her.

"Stop!" Babs commands, turning all her attention to the creeping vines. "Cease!"

"Now!" I nudge Jack, and he seizes his chance. I pull Kit behind me and jump up with my branch. Taishi scoops his branch up from the floor, where amazingly it hasn't been swallowed beneath the viney carpet, and together we swing wildly at the pirates who are now losing their footing on the unsteady floor, the vines wrapping themselves around their ankles and knees. The books and ornaments that they pulled from the shelves are floating on the vegetation, tilting and pitching as though they're on a heaving sea.

"Ha!" Jack shouts. He leaps from the bed, diving past the distracted crewmates and, quick as the lightning Babs is unable to summon, snatches the jaguars from the witch's hands and tears towards the door.

"NOOOOOOO!" Babs roars wildly. Without one look at her panicking, flailing crew, she deftly springs over the writhing floor and runs after him, shouting unintelligibly as she goes.

Taishi jumps on the bed, and Piper teeters on books like stepping stones, avoiding the snatching hands of the pirates. Together we watch as Neeves, Critchell, and Big Briggs are dragged through the wallpaper. Peg-Leg Pedro, who has been unconscious since Piper knocked him out, opens his eyes as the vines wrap around his arms and waist. As he is pulled backwards, his mouth is wide open in shock, but since his face goes through the wallpaper first, we can't hear what he says, and the look on his face makes Kit laugh out loud. As soon as the last pirate has vanished through the shimmery membrane, the rain stops and the room goes silent. All we can hear is the *drip-drip-drip* of water falling from the curtains, and all we can see is the faint movement of the leaves in the wallpaper, as the now-blue pirates are dragged deep into the depths of the jungle. Above us, the clouds have faded to white, although the ceiling doesn't look exactly like paint any more.

Taishi looks extremely satisfied.

"Do you think they'll be able to get out of the wallpaper again?" Kit asks, watching as the last leaf shivers and then goes still. "What if they manage to escape the vines?"

I shake my head and get to my feet, stepping onto the now-still floor. "I'm pretty sure that the house won't let them back out," I say. "I think they'll have to spend the rest of their days roaming the jungle, trying to escape from whatever blue and green animals there are in there."

"That's not all there is in there," Piper says mysteriously, patting her pocket. "I'll show you once we've got Jack. Oh - and there's something else awesome that I have to show... oh, there's not enough time!" She darts to the door and spins around impatiently. "Come on, we'd better run! I promise I'll tell you everything later!"

"How come they could get through the wallpaper, though?" Kit asks, climbing down off the bed and rushing after Piper, who has disappeared around the door. "Babs couldn't, earlier on, when she was touching it."

"I think that's your house," Taishi says, jumping down and catching up with him. "It's amazing. Piper, what did you find?"

I whip around the doorframe after them all, Silver darting around my feet.

Piper is up ahead and ignores Taishi's question. "Hurry up!" she snaps.

"I asked Merryshields to help," I tell Taishi and Kit, as we run towards the stairs. "Just before you and Piper got back with the vines. That was a brilliant idea, by the way."

"I wasn't expecting them to work on their own!" Taishi says.

"We'd better sprint," I say as I remember that Jack is on his own with Bad Babs. "Come *on!*"

Back To The Island

Jack

I run like the wind all the way back up the stairs and along the corridor towards the island room, my heart pounding in my chest and the jaguars getting heavier and heavier in my hands. They must be solid gold. Behind me, Bad Babs is roaring. Her footsteps slap wetly as she tries to keep up with me. I'm dripping wet too; I bet I'm leaving an easy trail for her to follow. I glance behind me once and see that I am quite far ahead - but not far enough. She is determined. She has one hand in front of her and it looks like she's trying to summon her magic again, only nothing seems to be happening. There are no clouds above her and I wonder for a moment if it was truly her magic in the jungle room, or if it was something to do with the house.

It doesn't stop it being scary, though.

The island room door is propped open with a rock and I hurtle through it at full speed, silently thanking Two-Legs for his foresight. The sudden bright sunshine blinds me for a second and I blink hard to clear my vision, the plan racing through my mind. I need to run to the trees - where hopefully I can lose her - then double back on myself and back get out through the door before she reaches me. I only hope Two-Legs won't get trapped along with her; I didn't see him in the corridor. I sprint for his and Taishi's campsite and then duck behind a boulder to catch my breath and peek behind me.

Against a tree are two tied-up pirates. They are struggling against their ropes, but are tied so tightly that they can't get themselves free. It must be Two-Legs's work, but there's no sign of him anywhere. Hopefully, he's back in the apple tree room - although something tells me he wouldn't just be waiting around, hiding, if he thought we might be in trouble. Before I can consider this, though, Babs emerges through the door and onto the sand.

If I thought she looked angry down in the jungle room, it's nothing to how she looks now. She is absolutely raging. Her hair has come loose and is flying around her face, even though there's no wind. Her whole body looks rigid with fury and as I watch, she throws her head back and howls up to the sky. The sound makes my skin crawl. Then she lifts her arms and I see the wind pick up around her, twisting faster and faster - like in the jungle room, only much, much worse. I guess Merryshields can't stop her magic as easily when she's on the island. Clouds build in the sky, and in seconds the sun is hidden behind the massive bank of a thunderhead, bearing down heavily over the island. I can feel the pressure falling.

"I'll get you, boy!" Babs screams, her voice shrill over the rising winds. With the clouds seeming almost at her shoulder, she puts her fingers out in front of her and begins to walk purposely straight in my direction. To my horror, she kicks the rock out from the door frame as she moves away from it, letting my only way back slam into non-existence. I'm trapped!

The jaguars twitch in my hands.

Making a split-second decision, I turn and sprint towards the window, along the quick route from the campsite to the clearing. My only hope is that Johnny Two-Legs hasn't got to the window yet and it's still open. I don't know what I'll do if it *is* there, since the climb would be beyond dangerous now the guttering is gone, but if it *isn't* there...well, then I'm trapped on a desert island with a witch-pirate who's really, *really*, angry.

The jaguars twitch again, and I wonder if that is a result of her getting closer. Can the gold sense her, too? Fat drops of rain are splatting down around me. I run harder along the sandy grass, ducking in and out of the leaves and bushes, and then there's a movement in my hands that can't be ignored. Almost tripping over tree roots, I hurtle towards the little clearing and look at my hands.

The jaguars...the jaguars are alive!

They're small, but they're growing rapidly. This is incredible! They're stretching and flexing their muscles, and their golden fur is warm and soft. I stumble into the space where the window used to be, still looking at the astonishing, scaled-down cats, and swear, very loudly, at the empty air where the window used to hang.

It's completely gone.

There is no sign at all that a window ever hung in mid-air there. Johnny Two-Legs must have done exactly what he said he would, and used some string to fasten it shut. Where *is* Two-Legs? I shuffle backwards, not knowing what on earth to do next.

The jaguars decide for me. They are too heavy to hold in my hands, so I place them gently on the sand. They are perfect miniatures and amazingly cute - or at least, they would be, if I didn't suspect that they were about to grow into huge, powerful, man-eating big cats. They stretch their slinky backs and then, to my surprise, they both blink and yawn and - *POP!* - their emerald eyes fall out! As they blink more, I see that they both have normal, dark cat eyes - as normal as can be for animals that are still golden, that is.

I'm transfixed. I can hear Babs moving through the undergrowth, shouting threats and curses at me. Making another fast decision, I leap forward, scoop up the four big jewels and clutch them tightly in my fists, and then I turn and run - straight into Johnny Two-Legs.

Two-Legs is looking a little the worse for wear. He is limping worse than usual and has a black eye and a ragged piece of material tied awkwardly around the arm that doesn't have the hook. His parrots are circling close to him, almost as though they are worried about him, too. But he's grinning, and he gives me a quick, strong hug before pushing me behind him. Bad Babs Bembridge has entered the other side of the clearing.

She stops at the sight of the golden jaguars, who have now reached full size and are prowling around the perimeter of the clearing, their gold fur going dark in splotches where the rain is landing. Her face lights up with greed.

"That hog-sweating journey was worth it, after all," she says.

I shuffle backwards along the sand. Something about the eerie, thundery atmosphere doesn't feel right at all.

"Good idea," Johnny Two-Legs mutters, limping backwards besides me.

Our movement catches a jaguar's eye. It pauses and makes a low-pitched growl. Babs looks straight across the clearing at us.

"Oho, you two maggots," she says, with an evil smile. "You think you can put me to all that trouble, just for me to let you walk free? Think again."

She flicks her wrist, and a bolt of bright white lightning shoots out from her fingers, catching the low branches of the tree beside me. I jump about a mile in the air. So do the jaguars.

"Be damned, woman, he's just a boy!" Two-Legs yells, putting his arm out in front of me. To me, he whispers, "Run, lad!" but there's no way I'm leaving him here.

Babs lifts her wrist again, but the jaguars growl at her.

"I'll knock you two creatures out as well," Babs spits at them, and lifts both hands up. "You're no good to me alive, anyway."

Thunder rumbles and I grab hold of Two-Legs's arm, wondering how on earth I'm going to get both of us back to the door before Babs strikes us down.

"Come on!" I say, pulling him backwards. Before we've taken a step, though, the witch has flicked her wrists and lightning has once more fired across the clearing at the jaguars - *but they are completely unharmed!*

And not only that... now they're angry.

Johnny Two-Legs finally moves.

"Feels like a hurricane brewing," he says.

"You think?!" I say.

Babs is spluttering and flicking her wrists, but although the lightning is spurting out, the jaguars keep advancing towards her, completely unaffected. "What? What?" she repeats, backing away from them as they stalk steadily onwards.

"Come on!" I say, not wanting to wait and see if she decides to send another blast of lightning our way instead. Johnny Two-Legs turns, and as we hurry as fast as he can manage down the narrow track that'll take us to the beach, I look over my shoulder to see Bad Babs scampering away as fast as she can in a different direction, jumping over tree branches and ducking under leaves. The two big golden cats follow her casually, cold intent in their eyes.

"Right you are, lad," Two-Legs says, after a quick look over his own shoulder. His parrots are fluttering, their wings working hard against the stormy wind. "Time to get a wriggle on. Come on, birds. Behopes that door of yours is still open."

"Behopes the others have made it back there," I mutter.

Jaguars and A Mango

Piper

W e race as fast as we can from the jungle room to the island, Silver barking urgently at our heels.

"The door's closed!" Willow gasps.

"Open it!" Kit yells, and I slam myself into it and turn the handle. No matter what is happening there, we can't leave Jack trapped.

The island looks like a different place to the tranquil, sunny beach we saw when we first opened the door, the day we'd seen the flag from the orchard. The sky is wild, filled with furious, heavy thunderclouds, and the palm trees are bending so far their leaves are touching the ground. The sea is roiling and boiling, as dark and grey as iron, and over the middle of the island there are flashes of lightning striking down wildly.

"That's Bembridge!" Taishi shouts. His face is full of fear again. "Johnny's in there somewhere!"

"So is Jack!" Kit says, and I have to hold him back from leaping over the threshold. Even Silver is staying back, scared by the unnatural weather. His tail is tucked right under his legs and he cowers by Kit's feet.

"No!" Willow cries, gripping the doorframe. "Piper, what do we do?"

I can't tell you how grateful I am that at that moment, Jack and Two-Legs appear from the other side of the door.

"Quick," Jack says. He is sweating, despite the wind and the fact that there's no sunshine. We scurry out of the way and the two of them collapse through the door and I slam it closed. Immediately, the sound lessens. We can still hear the waves crashing, but it sounds like someone's watching tv in another room, rather than being just the other side of a thin wooden door.

Willow puts her hand on it.

"I can still feel the wind pushing against it," she says anxiously. Taishi reaches into his pocket.

"I'll see to that," he says, and ties the string onto the handle, then winds it onto a handy nail that I realise has appeared in the wall. He's wrapping and knotting it so tightly that not even a hurricane could blow it open again.

"Thanks, house," I say. "That nail's perfect." I look round at them all, and wonder if now is the right time to tell them I found something special in the jungle.

"Where's Bab's now?" Kit asks. He's sitting on the floor, cuddling Silver.

Jack is flat on his back on the floor, breathing heavily.

"Trying not to be eaten by wild jaguars," he says.

"I *knew* they were going to come to life!" Kit says. "I saw them blink! Are they still gold, like Silver is still silver?"

"They were a sight to behold," Two-Legs tells him, stroking the red head of one of his parrots, which has landed on his shoulder. "Two full-size, pure gold jaguars, strolling around, live as anything."

"I wish I'd seen that," Kit breathes.

"Well, *I'm* glad we don't have to watch them eat Babs Bembridge," I say. "Even if she is a witch. So-"

"Me too," Willow says fervently, though the boys look like they disagree. "It's enough to know she's never going to harm anyone else, ever again."

"Is that door *properly* closed now?" Kit asks, as Taishi tucks in the last end of the string.

Two-Legs nods solemnly. "Closed as tight as can be. Nothing'll undo Taishi's knots."

Taishi doesn't speak, but the back of his neck flushes with pleasure.

"And I did that window meself," Two-Legs adds. "So you don't need to worry about that, either."

"It's a shame about the jaguars," Willow says. "Not staying gold, I mean. That would've been useful for the Olds, for the roof."

"And old Great-Aunt Glynis's downstairs bathroom," I agree. "But-"

"I don't want to live in an ordinary house," Kit says suddenly, sitting up straight with a worried look on his face. "What if Silver only exists *in Merryshields*?"

I have to admit that the thought makes me pause for a minute. "Don't worry," I start to tell him, but Two-Legs speaks over me, still thinking about the treasure.

"It is a shame," he says. "I don't know anything about your little dog, but as regards the jaguars, I reckon your parents could've got a pretty penny for those two. I'd wager gold is worth plenty no matter which world you're in. You'll just have to go back to your searching."

Jack pushes himself up and shakes himself off. He is still soaking wet - we all are - but now he's grinning.

"We might not have the jaguars," he says. "But we've still got treasure."

"What?" I say. Did Jack find one too?

"Well," he tells the group, slowly. "When I got to the clearing, where the window was, the jaguars' eyes fell out."

"Eeew," Willow squeals, squeezing her eyes shut.

"No, it wasn't gross, they weren't real," he laughs. "When I was running, their bodies came alive under my hands and I could feel their muscles moving, and they sort of... grew. Obviously, I put them down in the clearing - Willow, you would've loved them, they looked so cute when they were small. But their eyes - you saw they were emeralds? I got them."

He says it casually, but I can tell he's really proud of himself - the tops of his ears are all pink.

"What do you mean, you got them?" Taishi asks curiously.

"I jumped into the clearing and picked them up, before Babs got there," Jack says. "It was nothing, really," he adds modestly, which is very unlike Jack. "Any one of you would have done it."

"That's amazing," I say sincerely. "You really are the best runner. I'm glad it was you and not me."

Jack glows.

"Show us!" Kit says, and we all shuffle closer as Jack holds out his hand and uncurls his fingers.

In the palm of his hand lie four glistening green jewels, as big as grapes, as clear as glass, with a purple fire deep inside that flickers as he moves. I can't speak for staring.

"They're incredible!" Kit gasps.

"They're *valuable*," Johnny Two-Legs says. "Your parents will be able to fund all manner of projects with that. Buy a bit of a ship, that would."

"I've seen one of those in a king's crown," Taishi breathes, leaning on Two-Leg's shoulder to look more closely.

"Is it enough for us to stay at Merryshields, do you think?" Willow asks. "I mean, it's not just Auntie Glynis's downstairs bathroom, is it? It's the roof and all the other stuff, too. Surely these little things can't fund all that." She smiles apologetically at Two-Legs as I take a jewel from Jack and hold it up to the light, marvelling. "Not in our world, anyway," Willow finishes.

"I don't know," I muse. "I don't know how valuable jewels are, to sell them, I mean. But if you add *this* to the equation..." I put my hand in my pocket and pull out the thing I found in the jungle, and everyone gasps afresh.

It's another golden ornament, and the gold looks pure and shiny; the goldiest gold I've ever seen. What with all the drama, I haven't had a chance to look at it properly, and I'm pleased that it's still as amazing as I thought.

"A mango!" Taishi says. He looks delighted, and I put it into his outstretched hands. "We grow these in our village at home! They're delicious," he adds, and his stomach gives a grumble so loud that it makes us all laugh.

"Mum gets them sometimes," Willow tells him. "Where did you find it, Piper?"

"When I was following Taishi through the jungle," I say. "When we went to get the vines, I saw it glittering off to one side. There was a huge mango tree, amongst all the other trees, but this one was sparkling in the sunlight. That far into the jungle, everything was kind of an ordinary colour again, so I could see immediately that this one was gold. So I just..." I shrug, and smile at the glittering fruit in Taishi's hand, "I just plucked it straight off the branch."

I look round at the crew. Everyone is smiling. I sigh happily, and then my tummy starts to gurgle. I put my hand on it. "Sh," I tell it, and the others laugh.

"What time is it?" Jack asks, and then looks at his own watch. "Lucky it's waterproof. I don't think I've ever been this wet before."

"I *knew* you didn't wash," Willow says.

Kitchen Feast

Kit

S ilver's tummy makes a gurgle that I can feel underneath my hand, and my tummy makes one back. It's like our tummies are talking to each other.

"Please say it's lunchtime," I say to Jack. "I didn't realise it before, but I'm soooo hungry!"

"It's *way* past lunchtime!" Jack tells me. "It's half-past two!"

"I can't believe I'm saying it," Taishi says, looking at the golden mango in his hand, "but right now, I'd rather have a real one than a golden one!"

Piper takes it from him and puts it back in her pocket. "Shall we go and see if the kitchen has forgiven us yet?"

"It forgave us ages ago," I remind her, getting to my feet and stretching. "Me and Taishi will scout ahead if you like and make sure the coast is clear?"

"Good idea," Piper says.

"I wonder if Mrs B will be there?" Willow asks, as me and Taishi start off down the corridor.

"I'll just take it steady behind you," Johnny Two-Legs calls to Taishi, stretching his legs with a groan. "Bit more stiff than I used to be. Come on, you three," he adds to his parrots, who are flying along the corridor.

"We'll walk with you," Jack says to him. "Go on, Kit."

"I'm already going!" I say. "We'll see you down there."

We run to the kitchen, Taishi marvelling at the size of the house all the way down, and me checking every corner before we went round it, in case the Olds were roaming around anywhere. Luckily we don't see them anywhere, and when we get to the kitchen Mrs Boudry is there! And the entire kitchen is *filled* with food.

"It's like a party!" I say.

Silver skitters towards her, wagging his tail excitedly. He looks completely back to normal, thank goodness, and not scared at all. I think dogs must forget more quickly than humans about being frightened.

"Sit," Mrs Boudry commands the dog, and he does - just about. His front paws are tapping in excitement, and as she reaches down to pet him, I swear I can see him smiling.

"Is there a feast?" Taishi whispers to me. I look questioningly at Mrs B.

"A feast for the lot of you," Mrs Boudry replies, beaming at him with her smiley round face. "Quite a day you've had! Now, you two, make yourselves useful. All these plates here," she indicates the counters piled high with delicious-looking goodies, "can be put on the table, ready for when the others get here. And don't forget to *wash your hands*!"

We both look at our hands. I have to admit; they look a bit disgusting. They are covered in grime and dirt. I'm actually quite happy to get them clean. Taishi stands beside me at the sink, and when we've both made the biggest soap bubble we can, we move the plates of food onto the table. There are two different kinds of pie ("Chicken!" says Taishi, smelling one. "Mince and onion!" I say, peering at mine.), an enormous loaf of white bread with oats on top, little colourful dishes full of pickles, a bowl of cherry tomatoes, a dish full of golden butter and a jug of some fizzy pink liquid. Even the salad looks appetising: it has crunchy lettuce, cucumbers, thin slices of bright peppers and pink radishes sprinkled over the top. And that's just part of it!

"We should wait for the others," Taishi says, as we sit down. I have already reached for a piece of bread.

"Really?" I say, and at that moment, the others *finally* arrive.

"Taishi said we should wait for you," I say.

"We'll wait for Willow too, then," Piper says, making me groan.

"Where even is she?" I ask. "My tummy is *completely empty*!"

Willow appears before anyone can answer me, red-faced and out of breath.

"Well, you'll be pleased to know that the Olds are their same grumpy selves, stuck up in the Office Wing. So we'll be fine here for a bit. Johnny, you can sit here." She pulls out a chair for the pirate and he sits in it, looking slightly overwhelmed at the variety of food.

"Bit better than fish and coconuts, eh boy?" he says wonderingly to Taishi. He takes a small pot of seeds and sprinkled them on the floor, and his parrots all swoop to the ground and peck happily.

Taishi is grinning. "The lady had it all spread around the kitchen," he says, waving his arm to encompass all the many work surfaces. "She told us to bring it all to the table and by the time we'd done that, she was gone! Like she'd just vanished into thin air!"

"She probably did," Piper says, sliding into the seat opposite me and pulling a blue-rimmed plate off the pile. "I'm so hungry! I didn't realise how hungry I was until I saw all this food." Her tummy rumbles again and Willow smirks.

"*We* all realised how hungry you are," she teases, but Piper is glancing around the kitchen. I guess she's looking to see if Mrs Boudry is going to reappear anywhere, but there's no sign of her.

"She said something about laundry," I say. "She sounded a bit cross, actually. Said she couldn't get it done, something about new technology not being worth the paper it's written on or something."

"Ha! Auntie Percy said the same thing about that washing machine this morning!" Jack says through a mouthful of freshly-baked bread. "She was getting really cross with it."

"Mrs B has *completely* outdone herself this time," Piper says, piling her plate high. It's quiet for ages while we enjoy the delicious food, but eventually Two-Legs pushes his plate away and lean back in his chair. "I can't eat one more bite," he says firmly.

"Me neither," Jack says, doing the same.

"You don't want one of these fairy cakes, then?" Willow says, producing a plate that from behind the salad bowl that is stacked high with the little cakes. Each one has icing as green as the jewels in Jack's pocket.

"I think I've got a special space in my stomach for cake," I say, taking two and putting one on Taishi's plate. "These remind me of the emeralds. What shall we do with them?"

"That's what I was thinking about," I say.

Piper fills up her and Johnny's glasses with more fizzy pink juice, while Jack gets himself another piece of bread - so much for being full.

"First off, I think we should give two of them to these two," he says, looking at me, Willow and Piper. At our enthusiastic nods, he pulls the stones from his pocket and pushes one each into Taishi's and Johnny's hands.

"We can't possibly take these from you," Johnny protests, trying to hand it back again, while Taishi simply stares at his, glowing in the centre of his palm.

"You have to," Piper says firmly.

"We insist," I say.

"We couldn't have done all of that without you," Willow says, handing a piece of chicken from his pie down to Silver, who is going round the table to each of us. "And we've still got two, *and* Piper's mango. So there."

Johnny blinks for a few seconds, and Taishi closes his hand tightly over his emerald.

"Thanks," he says, his voice a bit husky. "It... thank you."

"You've made a great big difference to our lives, and that's the truth," Johnny says, looking at each of us in turn. "We'll never be able to thank you enough for saving us from that island, or for seeing to old Babs. We shall remember you forever."

Nobody quite knows where to look and we all grin and pay close attention to our plates, until Jack hands us each another cake. He raises his in a toast in front of him.

"Cheers, and here's to many more adventures," he says, and we all raise our cakes and laugh.

I remember something that was puzzling me. "How come you didn't come straight back through the campsite, if you were at the window clearing?" He looks confused for a second. "I mean," I say, "it's quicker than coming round by the beach."

"We *had* to come the beach way," Jack tells me, swiping a bit of icing off his cake with his finger. "I ran the campsite way *to* the window clearing when I first got on the island, but then Babs and the jaguars were blocking the clearing, so we had to come the long way back, along the beach."

"That's why we couldn't see you when we opened the door," Willow says. "You were *behind* us."

A funny sort of shiver goes over me. "Do you realise," I say, "that to get to the door, you probably walked *through* us?!"

We all digest that for a moment. Willow and Piper look a bit disgusted, but I can tell that Taishi thinks that's as cool as I do.

"Through us," he repeats, grinning at me.

"I can't make head nor tails of it, meself," Two-Legs admits. "But it's a good job you opened that door when you did. That hurricane of Babs' wasn't going anywhere."

"Have you seen her do that often?" Kit asks.

"Not often, but once would've been too much," Two-Legs says, shuddering. He looks better now that we've eaten, though his bloodstained bandage reminds me he was injured. I get up and go round the table, touching his shoulder gently as Taishi starts to tell the others about jumping into the jungle and getting the vines.

"Johnny, do you want a clean top?" I ask tentatively. Piper hears me and nods.

"And the first aid kit?" she asks. "It's got clean bandages and things in," she adds, as he looks questioningly at her.

"Well, maid, I won't say as it wouldn't be marvellous to be clean and dry," he tells her, and grins at me. "But I can't think that you'll have anything to spare for an old fella like me."

"I have an idea," I say, going across the kitchen while Piper rummages in the cupboard for the first aid kit. "Just a minute."

This morning, when Auntie Percy had been complaining about the washing machine again, I had seen a cupboard with a whole load of stuff that definitely wasn't ours. I hadn't really thought about it at the time, but now I'm wondering if there's something useful in there for Johnny - after all, Merryshields does seem to have an incredible amount of stuff just lying around. I have a little rummage and come out with a blue shirt and a huge pair of what look like gardening trousers, that definitely aren't Dad's.

"Here," I say to him, seeing that he has moved to the sink and started reapplying his bandage. "These should keep you dry, at least."

"It's like being at home," Johnny says, beaming. "Clean clothes and a full belly. I could fancy I can even smell my Elsie's lavender bags."

Piper and I both take a big sniff.

"I can smell lavender too!" Willow says, looking up from pouring Silver a dish of water. I think of something else, looking over at my friend sitting next to my brother at the table.

"Taishi can share my clothes!" I say. "I've got loads of t-shirts and shorts. Lucky all my uncomfy smart stuff went in the river!"

"Great idea," Jack says, but Willow and Piper are looking at each other like they're thinking something different. I frown at them, but they don't tell me, so I sit down again.

"Um..." says Taishi. His fist is still clenched around his emerald but his eyes are flicking towards the bounty of food on the table.

"Help yourself," Jack says, grinning and patting his stomach. "I thought I was full, but actually I think I can fit some more in."

Taishi stands and peruses the food, his free hand hovering first over the bread and then over the plate of fairy cakes, as if unsure what he wants more. Eventually, he decides on both and stacks the cake on top of the bread in a weird sandwich-like stack.

Johnny Two-Legs emerges from the utility room, dressed in his new, clean clothes. "This is fine luxury, this," he says, holding out his arms and admiring his shirt. It is strange to see him not looking ragged and scruffy, although his hair is still long and normal, and with a parrot on each shoulder and one on his head, he is definitely still a pirate. I go back to the utility room and pull out a pair of shorts and a t-shirt for Taishi, who smiles in delight.

"My mum won't know what to think when she sees me!" he says.

I smile back, but I see a funny look cross his face as he walks away to get changed, and I wonder if he's thinking of his mum, now that he's finally off the island and free of Bad Babs.

Johnny has started whistling softly. He's filled the sink with hot, soapy water and the bubbles are piled high.

"Just going to put these in to soak," he says, clinking two of the empty dishes into the steaming water.

"Do you want some more to eat, too?" I ask.

"I wouldn't say no to another slice of pie," he admits.

I reach for the chicken pie and slide the last piece onto his plate, then add some salad and another thick slice of bread. Then he comes back, drying his hands on a tea towel, and begins to eat again.

"Time to fill ourselves up, Johnny?" Taishi asks, reappearing. You'd think he'd look like a normal kid, wearing my clothes, but in fact somehow he looks even more piratey - maybe it's the long hair or the bare feet, but he and Johnny both still look like they're part of a different world. Silver barks at them, surprising us all, and everyone laughs, and Willow gives Silver a stroke, and I sit back at the table, trying not to think that things are about to change all over again.

Dowsing

Willow

P iper and I keep looking at each other across the table so I know we're both thinking the same thing - that Johnny Two-Legs and Taishi won't be staying. They both look like they're from another world - quite apart from the practicalities of where they would stay (what could we possibly say to the Olds?) I get the feeling that they both want to move on. The air has a sort of hushed quality, now that we've all eaten, and the kitchen is quiet. We've stacked all the dishes and put them into the big Belfast sink, where they've sunk down under the bubbles, and Piper has wiped the table. There's still some food left, but I think we're finally completely full, and it feels like that bit at the end of the party where you don't want to leave, but it's home time.

Johnny stands up, stretching his legs, and as if an unspoken order passed between them, Taishi pushes his chair back, too, stuffing two more slices of bread into his pocket. He still has his hand closed tightly around his emerald. Johnny must have stowed his away somewhere - he's stashed all his and Taishi's old clothes into a worn leather satchel that Piper pulled out of a drawer in the utility room, so I'm guessing it's in there.

"Right, then, mateys," John says, looking round at us all. "I do believe it's time we were away."

"Away?" Kit asks, surprised. "Away where?"

Despite the sense it makes for them to go, it suddenly seems inconceivable for the house not to have Johnny Two-Legs and Taishi in it.

"I've not seen my Elsie in over two years," Johnny says, smiling. "I left home to go to sea, and she was going to her sister's to find work. I should have been back home with 'er within months, but of course we landed up on that island, so I had no way of even letting 'er know I was still alive. She'll think I've drowned, and I'd like to know if she's alright." He stops talking quite quickly and his eyes go shiny.

"Of course. We understand," I reassure him, catching Kit's eye across the table. My cousin is looking horrified - and sad. Silver puts his head on Kit's knee and gazes at him, and Kit looks down at his dog, stroking his silky fur miserably.

"My family will be waiting for me, too," Taishi says, one eye still lingering over the table. Without a word, Piper gets up and starts finding bags to put food in. Silver trots from Kit to Taishi, and nudges his leg until he bends down to fondle his ears. "But I don't know how we can get back from this world, Johnny? I mean..." He frowns and scratches his head. "It doesn't *feel* like the same place. Even if we were to get to the sea..."

"But," Piper says, her lip trembling as she fills the bags with all the leftovers from our feast, "will we see you again? Will you come back?"

"Of course we'll come back, if we're invited," Johnny says with a soft chuckle. "Not visit the folks who saved us from a lifetime of coconuts and fish on that island? Unthinkable. 'Course we'll come back, if we can find a way."

"Well, you're always invited," Piper says stiffly. (That's how she talks when she's trying not to cry in front of a grown-up.) "But, it's like Taishi said--how *can* you get back? Do you need to get somewhere? We're a long way from the ocean in this world, and we can't get you to the coast."

Taishi and John look at each other.

"I think we need water," Johnny says. "I don't know *why* I think that, but I have a strong sense that where there's water, there'll be a way through."

Kit looks at the kitchen sink, and I laugh. "Of all the weird and wonderful things in this house, Kit, I'm almost certain that the kitchen sink is not a portal to another world."

"You never know," Kit says stubbornly, but he stands up and walks to the back door, peering outside. "There are loads of watery places in the grounds," he suggests. "The ornamental pond, the stream, the lake - though we've never been there - and I think Dad said there's an old fountain somewhere."

"There's another pond in the courtyard," Jack adds. He's at the sink, filling two bottles with fresh water, and he has to clear his throat to speak.

"What about... behind another door?" I ask. I don't *want* to say it, after the drama of opening the *last* magical door, but it seems like the most obvious place to start.

"Can either of you girls dowse?" Taishi asks, looking at Piper and me with interest.

"What about boys?" Kit says indignantly. "*We* might be good at dowsing."

"Can you remember what dowsing is?" I ask him, as Piper hands me all the bags to hold while she goes for fruit from the fruit bowl.

He scowls. "No, but that's not the point!"

Taishi raises both hands to stop Kit saying anything else. "I didn't mean to offend you!" he says. "It's just that the only people who could dowse for water in my village were women. That's all."

"If you say so," Kit mumbles.

"I don't think either of us can do it," Piper says, looking interested. "At least we've never tried."

"Can only witches do it?" Jack asks, returning with the water. He puts the bottles on the table and puts on his thinking face. "It doesn't work the same in our world, I don't think."

"I *have* heard of people doing it," Piper admits. "Mum's told us about it, people use coathangers..."

"What? That's ridiculous!" Jack says, rolling his eyes.

"The women at home don't use coat hangers," Taishi offers. "And they aren't witches, either. They're just..." He lifts his hands helplessly. "Ordinary!"

Johnny is nodding. "Where I come from, the young maids just learn how to do it. That's not to say the lads couldn't learn, too," he adds quickly, looking at Kit and Jack. "It's just that the girls seem to pick it up quicker."

"Not surprising," Piper murmurs.

"I could try!" I volunteer. I shove the armful of bags and containers of food into Taishi's arms and roll up my sleeves. "What do you have to do?"

Johnny grins. "I'd think you just have to hold your fingers out, and..."

"...and try and feel the water," Taishi finishes. "It didn't look very hard..."

"Vibrations," Piper says helpfully. "Remember Johnny said that Babs Bembridge felt vibrations from the gold?"

We shudder at the thought of the witch, but I grit my teeth.

"Right," I say. "It's worth a try." I hold my hands out in front of me and close my eyes. "Be quiet and let me concentrate."

They all stand silently. I can feel Jack scoffing inside his head - he'd never believe in something as unscientific as this - but I ignore that and try and think watery thoughts. There's the strangest tingling in my fingers and I smile, though I keep my eyes closed.

"Is it working?" Kit asks.

"Sh!" says Piper. She puts her hand on my shoulder and squeezes. "You just concentrate and we'll follow you," she says. "It's the best idea we've got."

So they follow me like a game of Follow-The-Leader (only where everyone is keeping really quiet and at least four of us have our ears strained for sounds of the Olds approaching from any direction). I lead us out of the kitchen and down a narrow corridor that connects to a different part of the house, where there's a little warren of small unused rooms, dark and cold and damp-smelling.

"Are you sure you're not leading us somewhere creepy?" Kit says. He's trying to sound playful, but his voice falls flat in the moist, dank atmosphere.

"Shush," I say, listening to my tingly fingers. It's weird, but not unpleasant, and I feel like I could shake it off at any moment, if I wanted to. "We're getting closer," I tell them. We turn a corner. I open my eyes. "Look," I breathe.

Ahead of us, the small corridor is filled ankle-deep with water that has dripped down the walls from a leak in the ceiling that is so big, I can see bits of grey sky through it.

"Here?" Jack asks doubtfully. "Are you sure?"

"The lake would've been better," Piper says. She sounds disappointed. Probably because lakes are more dramatic or something.

Taishi leans over the puddled water and sniffs. "Smells salty," he says.

"Even a massive storm couldn't fill the house with *seawater*," Kit says excitedly. "We must be in the right place! Well done, Willow!"

I grin. "So... what now?" I ask Taishi and Two-Legs.

"I say we just... walk in?" Taishi says.

Johnny looks at him for a long moment and then nods. "Aye," he says. "Seems sensible. As sensible as anything else that has happened in the last little while." He looks down at Kit, who steps forward, lips pressed tight together, and hugs John Two-Legs tightly around the middle.

"It was very good to meet you," Kit says, voice muffled.

John hugs him back with his non-hook hand, blinking tears into his beard, and thrusts something from his pocket into Kit's hand. "And you, my young lad. You look after your dog, there." He bends down to scratch Silver's ears, then looks at each of us in turn before smiling broadly and taking a great step into the puddle. He stops to wait for Taishi.

"Well, thank you for everything," Taishi says. He gives Kit a one-armed hug and lets us girls hug him, too.

Jack holds out his hand, captain-style. "Come back any time," he says, clearing his throat, though the words still sound scratchy.

Taishi shakes his hand and grins. For the briefest moment, he looks as young as Kit and I feel somewhat protective of him. But then, he follows Johnny Two-Legs with a splash. "Woah!" he says.

"What?" asks Kit.

"It's...it's warm!" Taishi breathes. He and Two-Legs wade slowly through the water, down the corridor. "Look at that, Johnny! Can you see?" Taishi points towards the end of the corridor, which just looks dark and boring to us.

Two-Legs grins and nods. "I can see it, alright," he says, clapping Taishi on the back. "Looks like we're going home after all, my boy!"

"It's like Mrs B," Piper murmurs, as we watch them get further and further away, their voices becoming more and more distant, the parrots swooping and gliding through the air after them. "Getting see-through."

She's right. They are becoming fainter and we can see the walls through them now. Just before they reach the other end of the leaky puddle, they both turn for a final time.

"Goodbye!" they shout, waving. Their voices sound like they are a hundred miles away.

We wave back. "Goodbye!" we shout.

Then we blink, and they're gone.

There is a beat of silence. "That's that, then," I say, feeling curiously flat.

Kit examines the thing Two-Legs gave him. "It's a key ring," he says. "Looks like Two-Legs made it himself. It's got his three parrots on, look." He holds it out to show us, a little sadly.

"Well, we've still got this," Piper says, patting the golden mango in her pocket.

"That's true," I say, cheering up and pointing at Jack's pocket. "And those! Let's go and hide them straightaway."

Treasure Hunt

Jack

W e stand in the corridor for a few minutes more, to be absolutely sure that John Two-Legs and Taishi have gone. I spend most of that time telling Kit not to follow them and look through the portal.

"We've had more than enough adventure for one day," I say firmly.

"And imagine what would happen if the water on the floor dries up and the portal disappears with it?" Willow adds.

This makes Kit stop arguing immediately, thank goodness. I can't imagine having to explain to the Olds that on the one hand, we'd found treasure, but on the other hand, we'd lost Kit to another realm and there was very little possibility of retrieving him. It doesn't bear thinking about!

Suddenly, Silver slips free of Kit and bounces across the water, barking until our ears ring with the noise bouncing off the dank walls. Fortunately, it seems the house doesn't want him to go through it, because a huge spray of water surges up and splashes all over him, sending him whimpering and shivering back to Kit with his tail tucked between his legs.

"Well, it serves you right," Kit tells him sternly. "Thank you, house."

"Right," I say to everyone. "I think we should go and get changed, so we don't look like we went swimming in our clothes."

They all look down at themselves. Willow nods.

"I'm dry-ish around the edges," she says, "but I'm still really soggy in the middle."

"Me too," I say. My clothes are more damp than absolutely soaking, but the wind on the island blew sand all over me, and it's still stuck to all my clothes. I don't fancy having to explain that to mam - what on earth would I say?

"Ok," Piper says. "Let's run, before the Olds finish work - it can't be that long now until the end of the day? You know how mum likes to come out early and check on us."

I check my watch. "Not long," I agree, and without any more discussion, we race all the way back to our bedrooms and get changed as quickly as we can.

"It feels so nice to be clean and dry," Kit says.

"Just dry," Piper tells him. "Getting soaked by a magical thunderstorm doesn't mean you're clean."

Kit shrugs. "Near enough," he says. "We're going to Headquarters, right?"

I nod. Headquarters seems to be the best place to make plans.

"Where did all those cushions come from?" Piper asks as soon as we walk in.

"The apple tree room," I tell her at once. "I recognise that red one. But what are they doing here?"

"The house must have decided this room needed them," Willow says.

To be honest, the room looks a lot less bare with a bit of colour in it. There's still the massive beanbag that Kit dragged down the day he found Silver, and now there are another dozen colourful cushions of different sizes, piled cheerfully into a corner. It looks quite home-like.

"I wonder if there's anything new in the map book," Kit says, going straight to the table and pulling the book close to him. "It might give us an idea of where to put the treasure."

"Ooh, I'd forgotten about that," Piper says.

I sit next to Kit. At first, it looks like nothing much has changed, but then I see the palm tree has two small figures standing beneath it, waving as though they are saying good-bye.

I point this out to Kit, and he smiles.

"And look, now there are two jaguars," he says.

"Turn the page," Piper says. "Let's see if anything else has come up."

Kit turns the page, past the sketch of the front of Merryshields ("The parrots have gone!" Willow says sadly.) and onto the next.

"There's something there!" I say. "Look, it's..."

"A bird?" Kit says, sounding disappointed.

"A goose," Piper says. "And those funny little squiggles are musical notes..."

"Well, that doesn't help us much," I say.

"No offence," Willow adds quickly. "We don't want to seem ungrateful to the house!" she tells me.

"Fine," I say, and close the book. "Let's think this through. Number one: the Olds have to find the treasure. And number two: it can't be us who gives it to them. They've got to find it on their own. They should think we have nothing to do with it."

"Exactly," Willow says. "Where should we leave it, though? Back in the Jungle Room?"

I shake my head. "We've got to leave it somewhere we don't want to go exploring. Who knows what cool stuff they might find if they start looking properly?"

We frown at the thought of this. I can just imagine the Olds rummaging around the house in all the magic rooms, getting in the way while we're trying to explore.

"That's *everywhere*, though," Piper says. "There isn't anywhere that we don't want to explore!"

"What about their bedrooms?" Willow says. "Or anywhere in the Home Building, really? We already know there's nothing magic in any of the rooms we've been, you know, *actually living* in."

"That's true," I say, thinking hard. "Their rooms, our rooms, the bathroom, the family room...the little rooms downstairs where they were talking about putting Great Great Aunt Glynis..."

"Under a pillow?" Kit suggests.

Piper shakes her head and rests her chin on her hand. "Do you think we'll find a library?" she wonders pensively. "I miss books."

I raise my eyebrows at her - she's not being very helpful.

"How about we hide it all at the back of a cupboard?" Willow says.

"What if..." I say slowly, as the plan unrolls in my mind. "What if we put it in that box we found up there?" I point to the cupboard we found the empty box in. "And we put the box... I don't know... under a floorboard somewhere? There must be a loose floorboard in at least one of those rooms."

"There is!" Kit says, jumping up excitedly. "In the corner of the Family Room! Remember when we had movie night and Mum told me to sit still on the beanbag because it kept squeaking? So she made me sit between her and Dad instead? Dad said," Kit put on a deep voice, "'*The floorboards in this house are*-'"

"We remember," Piper says quickly, before Kit can repeat Dad's exact words. "That's a brilliant idea!"

Loose Floorboards

Piper

T he box is exactly where we left it, beside the key that we never found a door to, in the tall cupboard that we'd earmarked as a toy cupboard - back when we thought our belongings would arrive and didn't know that they were, at that very moment, sinking to the bottom of a river. At the very foot of it, tucked right at the back, was the wooden box that had been on the shelf when we'd arrived. Jack puts it onto the table and we sit down to examine it.

"Do you think they'll realise it's the same one?" Willow asks.

Jack shakes his head. "No way. I'd put money on it. For one thing, they weren't even in the room when we first found it, remember? They didn't come in until after we'd put it in the cupboard. But for another thing, they were so excited to finally be here that they wouldn't have noticed if a herd of elephants had been dancing on the table. If we'd been as excited as them, they would have called us hyperactive."

"They would have said we'd had too much sugar," Kit agrees.

"I've never seen them go that bananas, not even at Christmas," Jack continues. "They definitely won't think twice when they find it."

"I think you're right," I say. "Let's see the emeralds again, Jack."

He pulls them out of his pocket and puts them on the table between us all.

"They really are beautiful," Willow says, putting her chin onto the table to look at them straight on.

"I never understood why people thought stones were pretty," Kit says dreamily. "But now I do. It's like it's got a little flame inside; if you tilt your head, it changes colour."

We all tilt our heads to see.

"You're right," I say.

"Piper, will the mango fit in that box too?" Willow asks.

I pull the mango out of my pocket and put that on the table next to the jewels. It seems even more shiny than when I'd first seen it, glimmering brightly in the late afternoon light.

"Yes, just about," Jack says, placing it carefully into the box. The house seems to glow around us, the air humming with satisfaction.

I smile at the room. "Do you think Merryshields is pleased we're here?"

"Definitely," Kit says, kicking a ball that Silver has dropped at his feet.

"Funny to think this it used to be a jaguar's eye," Jack muses, touching the emerald stone gently with one finger. "Do you think-"

Before he can finish speaking, we hear a shout from the stairs.

"Kids! Come and wash your hands! Tea's ready!"

We all jump up, looking at each other in alarm.

"We haven't had time to hide it yet!" Willow cries.

"I'm still full from the picnic!" Kit moans, his hands on his belly.

"You did have about twelve cakes," I say, rolling my eyes at him.

"Hurry," Jack says, scooping up the emeralds and dropping into the box beside the mango. I take it from him and close the lid with a snap.

"I'll do it," I say. "Tell them...tell them I'm in the toilet or something. Make sure they don't come into the Family Room..." I'm moving towards the door before I finish speaking. "Go!" I hiss over my shoulder, flapping my free hand at them. "You need to distract them, just in case!"

Willow nods, and so does Jack, grinning.

"Come on, boy," Kit says to Silver. "Let's lead the way."

I watch them hurry off towards the family room and then race away in the opposite direction, knowing I can get there a different way. That's the good thing about living in a house like this - there is more than one way to get to a room.

Five minutes later, I am in the family room and I can hear the others making loads of noise as they wash their hands - they are doing a good job of distracting the Olds. I sneak across the room to the big beanbag Kit was sitting on the other night, and moving it to one side, I find the loose floorboard. Thank goodness the Olds haven't had the money to put carpet down yet.

The board lifts up easily, to begin with, but there's a point at which it's jammed and I can't lift it with one hand. I put the box down carefully on the floor and heave with both hands as hard as I can. It creaks alarmingly loudly as it comes away from the floor. I freeze and strain my ears. The noise from the kitchen doesn't stop, and now I can even hear Mum singing. I exhale and slide the box into the space under the floor before placing the board back on top. It protests with another loud squeak, and then I hear Uncle Peter in the corridor.

"Did any of you hear that?" he calls.

Swearing quietly to myself (which I can only do because the younger ones aren't listening), I fling the beanbag back into place and duck quickly behind the sofa, my heart pounding with adrenaline.

Uncle Peter appears at the door and stands quietly for a moment, looking around. Then he says, "There you are!" and I nearly jump up, but of course he isn't talking to me. Uncle Peter always talks to his phone as though it's a living thing. He says it's because otherwise he'd have to smash it, as it is so annoying. He leaves the room, whistling, and I breathe a huge sigh of relief before following him carefully, winking to the others as soon as I see them to let them know that everything went smoothly.

GEM-eral Success

Kit

W e eat tea as fast as we can, not that I'm hungry *at all*, but the Olds take ages and ages. Piper even starts the washing up to move things along, and then *Jack* gets up to help her dry, which is even more weird. But it doesn't speed anything up. If anything, it seems to make the Olds even slower! Mam and Auntie Percy try to remember something from when they were kids and it stops them from eating their sandwiches. Uncle Peter fetches more crisps out of the cupboard and keeps searching the fridge for something interesting to eat. On a normal day, we would have benefited from all the food going around, but today we refused everything. The Olds didn't even notice it was strange, which is RIDICULOUS because we ALWAYS accept extra treats.

Jack asks the room what film we're going to watch tonight, and when the Olds look confused, me and Willow and Piper tell them that they *definitely* agreed to a movie night (even though they didn't). So even though they can't remember saying it, they think they must have forgotten. The four of us cousins agree on which film to watch in seconds, which should have raised some eyebrows because usually it takes us ages to agree. But the Olds didn't seem to notice that, either! Finally, Auntie Percy suggests we make popcorn. Normally, we would have been jumping and cheering at that, but Willow only manages a quick, weak "Yay." The Olds look puzzled for a moment, so the rest of us quickly make a fuss to distract from Willow's lack of excitement; luckily, this relaxes them and stops them from asking questions. Mam jumps up to fetch butter, salt and sugar, and Auntie Percy starts talking about different flavours and they have a WHOLE CONVERSATION ABOUT IT...

It is *very* frustrating.

At last, what feels like HOURS later, we are all sitting together in the Family Room. It's odd when you think about it. There are all these massive rooms in this enormous building, but in the evenings the cosiest place to be is a small room which Mam says once belonged to the butler. Dad lights the fire and I sit on my beanbag. At a signal from Jack, I begin fidgeting, just a little bit. Just enough to make the floorboard beneath me creak annoyingly.

This is the tricky bit.

I have to keep the creaking up, but without doing it so much that I get told off for it. And Dad is REALLY sensitive to annoying noises when he's watching films.

Mam shoots me a few frowny looks at first and Dad shuffles uncomfortably, clearly trying not to say anything.

Then Piper says, "What is that creaking, Kit?!" I can tell she's trying to sound like her normal self, but she winks at me to let me know what she's doing.

"Can you move your beanbag?" Mam suggests.

I make wide eyes at Piper since she's the only one who knows exactly where the creaky bits are. She subtly points backwards with one hand and I shuffle the beanbag that way, sitting quietly for a minute. Then Silver gets up and turns round and round next to me to make himself comfy, which makes the floorboard creak over and over.

"Kit!" Dad says crossly.

I nearly say IT ISN'T ME!, but I remembered just in time that the Olds can't see Silver and change tack. "Sorry," I say. "I can't help it, honestly. Everywhere over here seems really creaky."

Willow pauses the movie. "Do you want to have a look, Uncle Peter?" she asks. "I mean, you might be able to fix *this*, right?"

Me and Jack hold our breaths. It's a pretty big risk, reminding Dad of all the stuff in the house that he *can't* fix, but I can see what Willow's trying to do. Things are getting desperate. Luckily, Dad loves Willow loads, so he just rolls his eyes a bit and heaves himself up.

"Let me at it, son."

I jump up out of the way and try not to look at the others. My heart is jumping excitedly.

Dad tosses my beanbag behind him. "Turn the light on, Seren."

Mam turns it on, and moves to crouch down by Dad.

"Look at the gap, Peter," she says. "This whole house is out of shape. That floorboard's stuck all along this side, look, but there's a big gap on the other. You could fit a coin flat down it."

"You could fit loads of stuff down it," Jack says, peering over their shoulders. "Books. Food for mice." He glances round at us. "Hidden treasure."

"Try lifting it," Auntie Percy says. "You might be able to realign it somehow." She lifts her feet up off the floor and curls them underneath her on the flowery chair they'd found in an upstairs room. "I was all prepared for mice in the house, but I'd rather not invite them right into the Family Room if we can help it."

"Yeah, try lifting it, Dad," I say.

Dad makes a face, but his fingers are already in the gap. "It's a bit stiff," he says.

"Pull harder, Dad," Jack says.

Dad *yanks* it upwards as hard as he can. Then his face changes. "Have we got a torch handy?" he asks, peering into the dark space.

Mam rolls her eyes. "On your phone, old man," she teases him, and unlocks his phone to shine the torch for him.

Auntie Percy gets up to look. I take her place in the flowery chair, next to Willow. My tummy is so full of excitement it has ballooned up into my chest.

"What's that?" Mam asks.

Dad pulls the box out and shows it to the room. "It's an old box," he says, and lifts the lid. I hold my breath. The whole room is so silent you could have heard a mouse fart.

"Oh my goodness!" Mam cries. "Oh! Oh my! Look! Percy, look at that!"

Dad lifts the golden mango gently out of its nest and holds it out for all of us to admire. After a split-second's silence, we remember to be very, very excited and amazed.

"Wow!" I shout. "Is that *real* gold?!"

"It's so pretty!" Piper cries, jumping up to stroke the fruit and looking as though she's never seen it before. "It's a mango, right?"

"Yes, that's right," Mam says, taking it from Dad and turning it wonderingly around in her hands. "Feel the *weight* of it, Piper. It's certainly gold."

Piper takes it carefully in two hands. "It doesn't look like it should be so heavy," she says wonderingly. I never knew she was such a good actress!

"You - look - Seren - look!" Dad splutters. He pulls the emeralds out of the box, his eyes wide. "Look at the *size* of these! They're - surely, it's not glass... What do you think, Percy?" He hands one to Auntie Percy, and she holds it up to the light to assess it.

"My goodness," she breathes. "It's like there's a tiny fire burning inside it...I've never seen anything like it! It must be an emerald, surely--or something equally valuable."

"Valuable?" Willow asks. "Is it, like, *actually* valuable? I mean, can you use it to buy stuff? To pay for the roof?"

We keep really still, waiting for an answer. The grown-ups exchange glances for a long minute, with all kinds of grown-up expressions on their faces.

"Yes!" Auntie Percy says, and bursts into tears. "Yes, I think we can!"

"So, we won't have to go and live with Great Great Auntie Smells-Of-Wee?" I ask cheekily. They're so stunned that nobody tells me off for it, but Dad nods and pushes his glasses up onto his head.

"I imagine we'll be able to move her in here, and put in a simple bathroom for her, if that's what you want, love," he says, catching hold of Mam's hand.

She looks at him, eyes shining. "It would solve so many problems," she says.

"MUCH better than moving to a tiny house," Jack declares. "That would be so boring."

"It doesn't mean we'd be able to stop working," Mam says warningly, putting her hand on my shoulder. "You'll still have to entertain yourselves quite a bit, until we get things up and running."

I try to look disappointed, but don't think I really manage it. Luckily, she isn't really paying attention. Her eyes keep going back to the mango in Piper's hand. Piper catches my eye and beams. I can feel the Olds' excitement building up as they realise the complete amazingness of finding this treasure.

We don't watch the end of the film. We cousins eat the rest of the popcorn while we watch the Olds jump up and down in a joyful frenzy. Mam can't stop smiling and Auntie Percy keeps sitting down and saying "I CAN'T BELIEVE IT!", then getting up again. Dad rings his friend and sends him some photos and they have a conversation about valuation, and then the adults sit very quietly, staring at each other for a long time.

"I think it's all going to be alright," Willow says as we take ourselves to bed a few hours later.

Piper sighs with satisfaction.

Jack yawns. "Now we can go back to exploring for *fun*!" he says happily.

"We can finally find out where that key leads to!" I say, scratching the top of Silver's head.

"Ooh, yes!" Willow says excitedly. "You can put it on the keyring that Johnny Two-Legs gave you!"

We reach our rooms, and I am just about to say goodnight when I remember something.

"Piper," I say. "Didn't you say you'd found something awesome?"

Piper's smile stretches enormously all across her face.

"You just wait until tomorrow," she says. "We are going to have the best adventure yet."

Acknowledgments

Many people have helped me bring this book to life, and I would have to write another book to name them all, so to save you all valuable time here are the highlights.

Thank you to:

Elanor Best, editor extraordinaire, who with clear vision, excellent judgment and some tough love helped me to craft a story that not only shines but actually makes sense!

Louise Prentice, cover artist, who listened to my blurry vision for the front cover and translated it into the gorgeous beauty you see today.

The RM Book Club, for book recommendations, non-book-related chat, and your continuing and unalloyed enthusiasm.

Becca, for knowing what to say when, and for always picking me up and helping to banish the demons.

Elish, for being excited for me and for daily reminders that everything is actually always alright.

Sunniva, for a thousand threads of conversation, support, encouragement, walks, discussions and half-finished sentences...

David, for decades (!) of steadfast support, for all the life adventures and for being my partner in all things. I love you.

Imogen, Eve, Freya and Brodie - without you, this book would not exist. Thank you for daily inspiration and endless love. This book is for you, with all my love.

Also By, Again

Chronicles of Merryshields Main Series
Merryshields: The Island In The Attic

Chronicles of Merryshields: Stories from the Journal
Willow & The Hot Chocolate
Jack & The Exploding Planet
Piper & The Secret Story
Kit & The Ice-Cream

Buy
here
or from any retailers!

Join the magic at

Chronicles of Merryshields Newsletter

www.merryshields.co.uk

To read more of the adventures of Merryshields, join the Chronicles of Merryshields Newsletter for magical updates and a FREE STORY from the journal!

Out now! Merryshields: The Island In The Attic

www.merryshields.co.uk